Also by Steve Brown

Black Fire
Radio Secrets
Carolina Girls
The Charleston Ripper
The Belles of Charleston

The Myrtle Beach Mysteries

Color Her Dead
Stripped To Kill
Dead Kids Tell No Tales
When Dead Is Not Enough
Hurricane Party
Sanctuary of Evil

THE PIRATE
AND THE BELLE

THE PIRATE
AND THE BELLE

Steve Brown

Chick Springs Publishing
Taylors, South Carolina

First published in the USA in 2008 by
Chick Springs Publishing
PO Box 1130, Taylors, SC 29687
E-mail: ChickSprgs@aol.com
Web site: www.chicksprings.com

Library of Congress Control Number: 2008904755
Library of Congress Data Available

ISBN: 0-9712521-8-1
           978-0-9712521-8-9

10   9   8   7   6   5   4   3   2   1

AUTHOR'S NOTE

ACKNOWLEDGMENTS

For their assistance in preparing this story, I would like to thank Sabine Avcalade, Mark Brown, Sonya Caldwell, Judy Geary, Sally Heineman, Missy Johnson, Jennifer McCurry, Kimberly Medgyesy, Mary Jo Moore, Ann Patterson, Allison Pennington, Stacey Randall, Chris Roerden, Robin Smith, Dwight Watt, and, of course, Mary Ella.

This book is dedicated to all the people who would have enjoyed ambling down the streets of Old Charles Town.

CAST OF CHARACTERS

The Belle Family:
Catherine: Founder of the family in America
Nelie: Catherine's younger sister
Denis: Catherine's husband
Uncle Antoine: Owner of Belle's Mercantile
Uncle Francois: Manager Cooper Hill
Marie Torquet: Orphan adopted by the Belle family

On the *Mary Stewart:*
James Stuart: former privateer, pirate hunter
Samuel Chase: quartermaster
Alexander: cannon master
Kyrle: helmsman

Other Characters:
Robert Johnson: Governor, South Carolina
Alexander Spotswood: Governor, Virginia
Charles Eden: Governor, North Carolina
Colonel William Rhett: local ship owner
Lt. Robert Maynard: Royal Navy
Susannah Chase: Samuel's wife
Julia: James Stuart's maid
Caesar: Belle family manservant
Rodney Wickham: stowaway

Pirates:
Blackbeard (Edward Teach)
Robert Winder
Israel Hands
Phillip Morton
And Major Stede Bonnet

We will build a city that shall forget its past.

—Nelie Belle

CHARLES TOWN
1718

ONE

The enclosed carriage stopped at the unfinished house on Meeting Street, and one of two smartly dressed black men climbed down from the driver's box and opened the carriage door. A delicate, white-gloved hand extended from within. Its owner was assisted to the street by the servant, who closed the carriage door, then hurried up the steps to ring the bell.

Behind the young woman, carts, carriages, pedestrians, and men on horseback jockeyed around the carriage now parked on the most westward of all streets of Charles Town. Meeting Street had formerly stood in the shadow of a brick wall surrounding the city, but that wall had been demolished, with the accompanying rush to build on the far side of the street, further adding to the congestion.

Men openly stared at the young woman standing at the door of the strange-looking house, one of the first buildings to go up once the wall had come down. She was dressed in the fashion of the day: knee-length gown, open in the front from below the waist, serving as the top garment over several petticoats reaching her buckled shoes. Her hair was hidden by a lappet cap, and over her shoulder lay a parasol.

The servant rang the bell of this house that had been built perpendicular to the street and only one-room wide, causing consternation among Charlestonians— not an unusual state when something goes against the grain of public opinion. Under its gabled roof, the street-side door opened onto a full-length porch, and from that piazza, a center door led to the interior of the house. The piazza's roof shaded its windows from the sun and its open windows allowed the winds from the southwest to sweep through.

When ringing the bell produced no answer, the black man looked to his mistress. She nodded, and he rang it again, pulling on a cord running through a hole in the door frame.

Still no answer.

"Perhaps with more vigor, Caesar," said his mistress.

Catherine Belle was a slender woman with pale skin, blue eyes, and raven black hair. Her clothing was from London and she issued her commands in French. She was nineteen years old and at the height of her powers.

The black man used his hand and hammered on the door. Suddenly, the door was jerked open and a black woman stood there, one hand in the pocket of her dress. This was Julia who ran this household, and though she was an African, she was not a slave, which is probably why she did not care to smile when addressing the young white woman.

"Yes, Miss Catherine, how may I help you?"

"I'm here to see Captain Stuart," said the young woman, speaking English with a French accent.

Startled, the servant stepped back, and Catherine took that as an invitation to enter the house.

It was not what Julia intended. "Miss Catherine, Captain Stuart gave specific orders about your family and this house."

"Yes," said the young woman, hurrying across the piazza, through the center door, and into the house where she stood at the foot of the stairs to the second floor. "I'm sure he did."

Glancing around the hallway where the odd piece of furniture had been stacked and mud tracked through, Catherine recognized the floor plan from what James Stuart had presented in his proposal of marriage. She would never condescend to live in such a house. It gave the appearance of cheapness. Her family owned an English-style manor house farther north on Meeting, and their house favored one of the homes her family had had to abandon in their native France. Catherine and her family were Huguenots.

Caesar followed the maid into the house and stood at the open door to the piazza. Catherine handed him her parasol.

"Miss Catherine," said the maid, "you must respect Captain Stuart's wishes."

"Drunk again, is he?" The young woman glanced up the stairs.

Much of the house remained unfinished, yet James Stuart expected a Belle from Paris to live in such tight quarters. Who cared about all the sunlight and the breeze flowing through? This place was more suitable for a man who planned to continue to sail the Spanish Main. So, instead of this house becoming the crowning achievement of James Stuart's portfolio, it revealed the Scotsman's indifference to his family's position on the social ladder. And although Charles Town was nothing more than an outpost on the Atlantic seaboard, people would soon care about that ladder. Everything always came back to that ladder.

"Well," said Julia, looking at the floor, "you and the captain did have . . . a disagreement."

Catherine laughed. "And Captain Stuart has been drunk ever since I rejected his proposal of marriage?"

Julia said nothing, only stared at the muddy hallway.

"I suppose my family should take that as a compliment."

And upstairs she went, knowing the larger of the three bedrooms was finished and might even include furniture. That should be a sight: a bachelor purchasing furniture without consulting his fiancée.

The maid raced after her. "Miss Catherine, you can't go up there."

"What you mean is Captain Stuart is not presentable. Well, I have nursed many a sick or wounded man in my short time in Charles Town, and there is little I have not seen."

"But Captain Stuart is a proud man. A Highlander." Julia caught up with her, reaching the second floor at the same time. "Please allow me to go ahead of you and wake him."

"If you must. If you can."

Catherine remained at the head of the stairs, one of her gloved hands gripping the railing while the maid hustled down the hallway. Glancing at Catherine from where she stood in front of one of the doors, Julia rapped fiercely before announcing herself and entering the master bedroom.

A roar from Stuart revealed he was not pleased to be awakened, and that was all a lady needed to know about James Stuart. Screaming at the servants. How lowborn.

As Catherine sashayed down the empty hallway, she removed one of her gloves. It would seem that the maid was having little success in raising the Scot, so before taking off the second glove she rapped on the closed bedroom door.

"Captain Stuart, this is Catherine Belle. Make yourself presentable. I am preparing to enter your bedroom."

Despite her tone, Catherine could not help feeling flush and a bit dizzy, and she placed her still-gloved hand on the unfinished wall to steady herself. The man was, after all, a brute, and exactly why she was here. Send a pirate to catch a pirate. It all made perfectly good sense to her.

But not to Uncle Antoine. Uncle Antoine had spent last night in his cups, bemoaning their fate. Catherine thought his concerns misplaced. Blackbeard had been very good for the Belle family. During the blockade, she had made one business arrangement after another, even one that might put a competitor out of business. As her father had taught her: Make the grandest plays when the streets run red with blood.

From inside the bedroom came pleas from the maid for Stuart to sit up.

My God, how drunk could the man be? Catherine had heard stories about drinking bouts involving sailors, and rumor had it that most pirates sailed around in a drunken daze, but . . . Stuart was a fool! While he'd been drunk, how much money had he lost? After all, those who ran his business were former pirates, too.

Catherine knocked again, then shoved open the door and entered the bedroom. There she found the servant trying to cover her master with a bedsheet.

"Leave me alone!" he shouted, trying to sit up. He stopped resisting when he saw Catherine enter the room. "You! What are you doing here?"

Stuart clawed his way to an upright position on the edge of the bed. Fortunately, all Catherine saw was a pair of monstrous white legs as he fought to sit up. Stuart wore only a shirt, which the maid quickly repositioned from where the garment had become twisted in his sleep. Brown hair stuck up at odd angles. Sleep lines crossed his sunburnt face.

Stuart lurched to his feet, and just as quickly, he gripped his head with both hands and returned to the edge of the bed. The maid hastily pushed the shirt down between her master's knees again.

"Leave this house at once." Stuart spoke French with a Scottish burr. "I will not have you in my bedroom or anywhere else in this house."

Catherine held her ground as she always did with the riff-raff of Charles Town, which included just about anyone on the peninsula. Less than fifty years ago, no white people had lived here, and *her* family was from

Paris. Who did these Charlestonians think they were? Indians still led packhorses loaded with deerskins into this so-called town.

"Captain Stuart," said Catherine, picking at the fabric of her still gloved hand, "I have come here with a proposal . . ."

Her voice drifted off as Catherine Belle, lately of Paris, realized that no drawings in any marriage proposal could have prepared her for this room: the delicacy of the molding of the bed and its matching furniture, the pale French wallpaper, the hand-made Persian carpet . . . That is, unless Catherine had forgotten the bedroom of her youth. She had not.

Nor had Stuart forgotten that she stood in his bedroom. "I want nothing from you or your family!" Standing again and taking her by the arm, Stuart marched her out of the room.

"You're hurting me," she cried out, knowing she would bear his mark for days, perhaps weeks. The man was truly an ogre.

"And my answer is 'no' to your counterproposal." Pulling her down the hallway, he added, "Just as your answer was to me."

Catherine struggled to shake loose, but the man was much too strong. "Captain Stuart, release me! Release me this very instant!" She was at the point of tears. No man had gripped her so—not since her escape from France.

At the head of the stairs, Stuart stopped. "Not until you promise to leave my house."

"You call this a house?" Gesturing with her free hand, she added, "This is no house. In Paris they know how to build real houses."

Stuart sneered at her. "One insult after another, is it? It's a wonder your throat hasn't been cut and you left for dead in some back alley."

Catherine jutted out her jaw. "Just your sort of contribution to this so-called city. Listen to me, you . . ."

The animal tried to drag her down the stairs, but she would not have it. Catherine had grabbed the upstairs railing, making it impossible for the pirate to pull her down the steps—not without both of them stumbling and falling.

Realizing this, Stuart stepped back on the landing and ducked under her arm. Suddenly, Catherine had her hand wrenched off the railing, and she found herself being carried down the stairs over Stuart's shoulder, petticoats flying.

"Unhand me, you brute!" With her hands free, she flailed at Stuart's back, causing little or no damage. Her feet, now in front of Stuart, kicked hard, but to no avail. Her purse slipped off her arm and fell to the stairs.

Caesar, who had remained at the entrance to the piazza, hurried to open the front door as his mistress was carried out and dropped, feetfirst, on Meeting Street. Her driver stared down at them, and the traffic slowed, some stopped, all staring at the young woman with the flying petticoats and the man wearing only a shirt.

Once her feet hit the cobblestones, Catherine straightened up to confront the lout, but all she saw was the dirty shirt, those powerful, white legs striding up the steps, and the door slamming shut. From inside, she heard a lock thrown.

"You fool!" she shouted. Catherine glanced at the people gaping at her from horseback, shank's mare, or their own carriage. Again she flushed and this time in rage.

"You drunken fool!" she shouted, knowing the door to the house had not yet closed and the windows of the piazza remained open. "My family will never do business with you again. You hear what I say, sir. You'll never do business with the Belles of Charles Town."

A lock was thrown, the door opened, and her purse flew out, landing at her feet. Catherine ignored the purse but felt the stares of those passing on Meeting Street.

She faced the gawkers. "Well, what are you staring at? You don't think a woman can give a man an ultimatum?"

It was only after she returned to her carriage and the carriage was moving down the street that Catherine realized she hadn't had a chance to tell the fool pirate that her sister had been kidnapped.

SCOTLAND
SEVERAL YEARS EARLIER

TWO

Contrary to what people believed, the mother of James Stuart did not have strong ties to the Highlands. As a young woman, she had been kidnapped from her Protestant family while they were farming in one of the valleys of central Scotland. When her Highland "husband" fell in battle during another raid, one in which the Highlanders were beaten back by a regiment of battle-hardened redcoats, the surviving members of the clan returned to the Highlands to lick their wounds and divide the surviving women. One of the women was Mary Stuart; her son to be raised by his Catholic uncle. But after serving the men more whiskey than they could hold, and tolerating being slapped on the backside and pinched and fondled, Mary packed a bag, grabbed her son, and fled the Highlands.

Mary, however, did not return to her home in central Scotland, but disappeared into the bustling city of Glasgow. In Glasgow, Mary found work as a barmaid and occasional whore, and for this reason,

THE PIRATE AND THE BELLE

James Stuart grew up on the water instead of in the Highlands and soaked up much more education than one would normally expect, as the Scots were among the most literate nations of Europe. After the Acts of Union joined Scotland and England, Glasgow became the center of trade with the Americas, especially tobacco from Virginia. But this new life came to a sudden end when one of his mother's lovers stabbed her to death in a jealous rage.

When James leaped to his mother's defense, the seaman, who outweighed the fifteen-year-old by more than a hundred pounds, picked up James and threw him out a second-story window, then returned to his bloody work. Leaving the scene covered with blood, the sailor thought the boy lying on the cobblestone street only merited another kick in the ribs.

The sailor should have killed him. James, first crawling toward the harbor, then assisted to his feet by horrified neighbors, caught up with the sailor as he strutted up the gangway and joked with his shipmates.

"You should see what the other bloke looks like."

Throwing himself at the man, the sailor and James fell into the harbor where the man's extra weight became a minus instead of a plus. James, the local champ at holding his breath underwater, drowned the sailor in the presence of his shipmates. In this, he was assisted by townsmen who threw cobblestones at the crew whenever one of them made an attempt to rescue their crewmate.

Still, there were consequences. The sailor's death left the ship one hand short in a harbor with little or no unemployment. So, without being given the chance to bury his mother, and wearing only the clothes on his back, James Stuart shipped out on a vessel involved in the Triangular Trade.

The first leg of the triangle sailed from a European port where copper, cloth, trinkets, beads, guns, and ammunition were ferried to Africa. Then, up one of the many rivers of Africa, that cargo was exchanged for slaves, tightly packed in the hold like any other cargo to maximize profits. The ship then journeyed along what was called the Middle Passage, and once the slaver reached the New World, the surviving Africans were sold for a tidy profit. A slave purchased for ten dollars in Africa could be resold in the New World for twenty-five.

But even before reaching America, James had already clashed with the ship's captain, as many fatherless boys do when they run into their first authority figure. James, now seventeen, was occasionally sent into the hold where the Africans were chained, cheek by jowl, and in the hold, James finally gave in to the mournful begging of a wretched-looking African shackled near the ladder.

"Water . . ." pleaded the man.

James knew feeding the Africans was against the rules. He also knew the Africans were allowed topside every few days to be hosed down with saltwater and given a cup of water and a piece of bread. Then, after being returned below deck, another group was dragged topside. A retaining wall between the helm and the main deck kept the Africans at bay; members of the crew armed with pistols or long guns stood guard on the other side of that wall. Nets on both sides kept the Africans from committing suicide by leaping overboard.

When James was caught smuggling water to the African, he and the black man were taken to the captain, who immediately slit the African's throat. The African's head was severed from his body and nailed to the mainmast, the body tossed into the hold, another stench adding to the many odors of several hundred men and women chained below. James was ordered to mop up the blood, and it took a great deal of time before the deck was cleaned to the captain's satisfaction. Then, the captain grabbed James by the collar and dragged him aft, where he prepared to fling the boy into the ship's wake.

Before he could, the quartermaster sidled up to him. "A word with you, Captain."

On a pirate ship, the quartermaster represented the interest of the crew to the captain; both positions democratically elected. The quartermaster also judged disputes and disbursed food and booty, and since this particular ship engaged in a bit of "freebooting" when times were slow, the lines of authority followed those of the typical pirate ship.

"Once I've disposed of this jetsam," replied the captain. He smacked James in the face so the boy would stop struggling. Blood ran from the corner of James's mouth and his world lost its focus.

"Sir, the boy is the reason for my query."

Bracing James against the stern, the captain inclined his head toward the young Scot. "You disagree with my decision?"

"No, sir, I do not. All challenges to authority must

be dealt with swiftly and harshly, but the boy suffered no failure of nerve as he bound wounds when we came under attack by those pirates leaving Africa. Even the ship's surgeon spoke of him in the most laudatory terms."

"So, he should be allowed to live and undermine my authority?"

"No, sir. He deserves the punishment you are about to mete out, but you know as well as I, pirates hover around our ports of call. Once we're in sight of the Charles Town Bar, I doubt anyone cares whether you toss him over the side or not."

FRANCE
JUST OUTSIDE PARIS

THREE

atherine Belle woke with a start.

When the door to her bedroom opened, she was already sitting up. The riots in Paris had conditioned her to wake at the slightest sound. Across the room lay her younger sister, Nelie, sleeping the sleep of the dead. Both girls slept in their dresses and both dresses were very black.

The figure spoke from the hallway darkness. There was no candle, no backlighting. "Catherine?"

"Yes, Papa." Both spoke French.

"It is time."

Though her father could not see her, Catherine shook her head. "Papa, I cannot do this. I cannot leave France."

"Young lady, we have discussed this many times before and this is the only way to keep the family together." He waited. "Or would you rather remain in France and join a nunnery?"

Catherine didn't know how to answer the question.

A devout Calvinist, becoming a bride of Christ seemed a reasonable option.

From the hallway, her father said, "Remember, Catherine, you and Nelie must make haste, not waste your time."

And her father was gone, his footfalls on the stairwell the only sound to be heard. Catherine was expected to get her sister out of bed and down to the carriage. It was a moonless night; as was the previous night when they had left Paris, and this was not Catherine's room but her sister's. Nelie's room had been chosen because it was the most convenient to the stairway leading to the rear entrance of their country house.

Catherine fell back on the bed. Tears formed in her eyes. She didn't want to leave France, but the King no longer wished them to be here, and for as long as Catherine could remember, Huguenots had been leaving France. Only the year before, Uncle Antoine had left with his son, Denis. Now it was her family's turn.

From the doorway came a hiss, startling Catherine into sitting up. "Make haste!" This from her mother, before she, too, went down the rear stairs.

Catherine wiped away her tears with bedcovers that would never cover her again and listened to her mother's hand scrape along the wall as she fumbled down the stairs. In the other arm, her mother held their baby brother and fed him at her breast. Tonight of all nights the baby must not cry, and for that reason her mother did not suckle the child earlier in the day, explaining to the servants that the baby was fussy because he was colicky.

Catherine slipped out of bed, fumbled around on

the floor, and found her shoes. She fit them on, laced them up, and got to her feet. She brought along her doll, though Catherine considered herself much too old for dolls. But she could never leave Bebe behind. Bebe had been with her ever since she could remember.

"One toy or book," her father had said this afternoon in the parlor, "and you'd best be able to carry it."

Neither Catherine nor Nelie liked this and they let their father know about it.

"Watch your tongue," hissed their mother from where she rocked the baby, trying to quiet him. "The walls have ears."

At fifteen, Catherine understood the concept, but her twelve-year-old sister did not.

"But why must we leave?" asked Nelie. "I have friends here."

With a quickness that startled both girls, their mother was out of her rocker and across the room to the settee where the two sisters sat, causing both girls to lean back.

Still, their mother whispered when she spoke. "Nelie, how many times must I tell you that when the family speaks among ourselves, it's family business, not the business of servants."

"But, Mama—" started Nelie.

"What is our destination, Nelie?" demanded their mother.

The girl blinked. "We are returning to Paris . . . after checking on the country house."

Satisfied with the thorough job of indoctrination that she and her husband had achieved, she gave her daughter a warm smile. "Yes, my dear, we are returning to Paris after visiting—"

"Anyone but Catholics!" spit out Catherine.

From a couch near the fireplace, her father chided her. "Rein in your bile, girl. There is more than one use for lemons."

Catherine stared at her father. There was a lesson to be learned here, but she would have to do the thinking. It was her father's way.

Beside their father sat their seventeen-year-old brother, staring at the floor. Her brother was smitten by the girl on the neighboring estate. Unfortunately, she was Catholic, and the Belles had forbidden their son to see her. The girl's family had reciprocated. Not that that deterred young love, and on more than one occasion, while Catherine sat in her window seat and stared in the direction of Paris, she'd seen her brother slip from their house and disappear down the road for a nighttime rendezvous.

"And because it is such a long trip, Nelie," continued her mother, straightening and rocking the baby who had begun to whine, "we must leave in the middle of the night."

"But, Mama, I have hardly seen anyone here in the country."

"Many of your friends are no longer here, my dear."

"But why . . . ?"

Their father rose from the sofa. "Nelie, have you learned nothing from the last few years? The destruction of our churches, the closing of the Protestant schools, not to mention we are only one step ahead of the *dragonnades*, who would certainly hang your brother and I, then send you girls and your mother to a nunnery."

Seeing the shocked look on his daughters' faces, Jean Pierre realized he'd gone too far. He gripped his son's shoulder and smiled down at the boy. "And this one . . . this one has his head in the clouds. There is little we can do for him."

Catherine's brother only stared at the floor.

Jean Pierre crossed the room and took his wife's arm, ushering her back to the rocker. "Really, my dear, I don't like to see any sudden movements on your part. Not in your condition."

His wife didn't appear to share his concern. "Everything is arranged?" she asked, retaking her seat.

"Everything is as it should be, my dear. Our home appears as other Huguenot estates: weeds grow everywhere and dust covers the furniture. Only two servants remain."

"I know about the dust," said his wife, bitterly. Tears formed in her eyes as she scanned the parlor with its fine furniture and beautiful appointments. "Must we leave everything behind?"

Her husband did not remind her that they had resolved this issue before leaving Paris, and upon arriving at their country estate, all Catholic servants had been dismissed. Tonight, they would travel to the port city of Calais, and from there, on to London, then Charles Town, following the example set by Antoine and his son.

When questioned about the English colony, his brother had only smiled and said, "Jean Pierre, all you need to know about Carolina is that the colonists are as warm as their weather."

Still, Jean Pierre had put off leaving France. The Belle family had been a part of France even before there had been a France. "Yes, my dear," he said to his wife, "everything must remain behind."

Returning to his seat beside his son, Jean Pierre attempted to lift everyone's spirits by telling them of the warm weather in Carolina, made even warmer by its inhabitants. Or, wondered Jean Pierre, would the girls prefer to hear why all those banknotes had been sewn into the lining of their petticoats? Let in on such a secret might finally make the girls smile.

Now, in darkness in Nelie's bedroom, Catherine felt her way across the room, found her sister's form, and shook her shoulder. The stays in the older girl's corset were stiff, so Catherine could hardly bend over, nor did the cut of her dress allow her to raise her arm above her shoulder.

"Go away," said her sister, rolling toward the wall.

Catherine shook her again, and when Nelie didn't respond, Catherine seized her sister's arm and pulled her from the bed.

The girl cried out when she hit the floor.

Catherine ignored her, demanding that she sit up and put on her shoes. "And stop making so much noise."

Sitting on the edge of the bed, Nelie said, "You are the meanest sister in the whole wide world."

Shoes were thrust into Nelie's hands.

"I shall give you one minute to put these on and then I will drag you downstairs by your hair."

Nelie looked around, puzzled. "Why are the lamps not lit?"

"Catherine?" hissed their father from the hallway. "Are you and your sister coming? If not, we shall be forced to leave without you."

Catherine returned to her bed, fumbled around in the darkness for Bebe, found the doll, and went to stand at the door. "Nelie, I shall count to ten."

It didn't take that long, for, in truth, Nelie had always been a quick learner. Once Nelie visited the chamber pot behind the privacy screen, she followed her sister into the hall, down the stairs, and out the back door where their mother and the baby waited inside the carriage.

Jean Pierre didn't wait for her to climb aboard but picked up the girl and placed her inside the carriage. He then returned to the harness to examine the horses, rechecking the cloths wrapped around each hoof.

Catherine, one foot still on the ground, watched the thoroughness of her father's preparation. Here was another lesson to be learned, but not by her brother who looked down from the driver's box. The look on his face was gloomy.

Once everyone was inside and the carriage under way, Jean Pierre said, "We must hurry. The remaining servants have left and someone may have raised the alarm."

From where she sat next to her mother, Nelie asked why the servants had left without preparing breakfast. Her mother uncorked a small bottle of wine and shoved it into Nelie's hands.

"Drink this. It will make you feel much better."

Across the coach, Catherine gripped her father's arm and leaned into him. Jean Pierre kissed the girl's forehead, then untangled himself from her, bent over, and began to fiddle with the flooring. As the carriage turned onto the road to Calais, a piece of flooring fell away. Beside the hole in the floor, Jean Pierre placed several dark blankets that had been stacked on the seat beside him.

"Oh," said Nelie, bending over and looking at the irregular shadows as they passed on the road below. "But why . . . ?"

"Drink the wine, child," said her mother, using her free hand to force her daughter to sit upright.

Nelie drank from the bottle and made a face. The wine had not been cut. The twelve-year-old was drinking Madeira straight.

Now the carriage picked up speed, and the family resisted one last look at the life they were abandoning; all except Catherine, who lifted the corner of the curtain for a final glimpse of a place that held such fond memories.

She was leaving more than her family's country house, she was leaving behind her childhood, and Catherine resolved that once she reached this colony named for the English king, that she would work without complaint to rebuild their lives. Even more than her brother, Catherine appreciated the gravity of her family's situation. For that reason, strung around her neck, but covered by lace and fabric, hung a good deal of jewelry. Her family would make a fresh start in the New World.

Catherine dropped the cloth and re-buttoned the window. Turning to her father, Catherine was startled to see him darkening her sister's face with a piece of drawing charcoal, then fastening a black bonnet on Nelie's head. Everyone was dressed as if they were going to a funeral, and they just might be. Finished with her sister, Jean Pierre colored Catherine's face with the charcoal and fitted a similar bonnet on her head.

Curse of the Belle family, thought Jean Pierre as he secured the bonnet under Catherine's chin. All Belles have blue eyes, black hair, and pale skin that never darkens, even during the sunniest months of the year.

He gestured at the hole in the floor. "My dear, do you understand why there's no bottom to the carriage and how you might turn that to your advantage?"

Instantly, all dreams of a new beginning fell away as if falling through the hole in the carriage floor. Catherine jerked her head in nods, remembering her instructions if the carriage were to be stopped. She trembled and could not speak.

Seeing this, her father drew her into his arms and whispered, "Always remember that when one door closes, another opens, and you, my dear, are just the sort of clever girl to learn where all these doors might lead."

"But why are we doing this?" cried Nelie from the other side of the carriage. "Why must we leave our homes?"

Her mother put her arm around her daughter. "Close your mouth around the bottle, dear. That will take all your cares away."

Nelie took another pull on the bottle and soon fell asleep. She never heard the demand for their carriage to halt.

"Highwaymen," said her father, dropping the piece of charcoal through the hole in the floor. "I'll handle this."

To his wife, he said, "You know what those blankets are for."

His wife glanced at Catherine and then clutched the baby. She could only nod.

Jean Pierre brushed his hands on his pants, stood, and opened the carriage door. But he could not move. Catherine had grabbed his arm.

"Papa, please don't go. I don't think I could bear it if you did."

From outside came a man's voice. "You inside the carriage. Everyone out."

Jean Pierre smiled down into the face of the cleverest person he had ever known, and Jean Pierre had met a number of clever people while living in Paris. Still, he would match Catherine's wits against those of any child of the most prominent families in Paris. It also meant that any hope of his line surviving rested on the shoulders of this fifteen-year-old.

He lifted Catherine's hand from his arm. "Remember your responsibilities, girl. Never forget your responsibilities to your family." And he opened the carriage door and stepped down into the face of several muskets.

In the driver's box, his son began to weep. It wasn't highwaymen that had stopped them, but the enforcers of the Catholic faith against recalcitrant Huguenots, the feared *dragonnades.*

FOUR

The day James Stuart was to be flung over the stern, he caused several members of the crew to chase him around the ship. Then, he scaled the rigging and refused to come down when ordered to do so by the captain. Teeth clenched on knives, three sailors started up after him, hand over hand. At the platform mounted on the mainmast, all the help James received from the lookout was a curse and a boot that came swinging toward his head. Panting from exertion and glancing at those climbing up the rigging, knives in their teeth, James knew it was time to go over the side. And over the side he went, sailing out over the deck and neatly slicing the surface of the water.

James held his breath and waited for the ship to pass. It did, but not before a few musket balls slashed into the water, white streaks ripping though the blue. James forced himself deeper, and when he could hold his breath no longer, he shot to the surface, gasping for air and looking around. He found the ship well past him, and the captain busy trimming its sails.

James looked toward Charles Town and doubted he could swim that far. The harbor appeared to be three or four miles away. Several small islands and sandbars lay to his left and right, but the nearest thing to him was a skiff from which an old black man fished. Since the boat was some distance away, James called to the man to bring the skiff closer. The fisherman didn't appear to hear him. When he couldn't get the man's attention, James started screaming and thrashing around.

The African lifted his head, covered by some sort of woven hat, and stared at him. Besides the woven hat, the African wore a long-sleeve shirt and pants to protect him from the sun. The fishing line remained in the water, and it took a moment before James realized the man would do nothing for him. But he just might drown if he continued to yell and thrash around.

James struck out for the boat, and, fortunately, the fisherman didn't row away. Still, it was a long haul, and James was so exhausted by the time he reached the boat, he didn't have the energy to climb over the side. And the sea had turned rough, waves slapping his face. The wind had picked up.

"Help me . . ."

The man ignored him, so James tried climbing over the side.

His hands were too wet and he slipped off the side and went under again. Arms limp, legs numb, James was tempted to give up. But if he had, he wouldn't have seen his angel float by.

James struggled to the surface, breaking into tears and grasping the side of the skiff. "Please . . . help me . . ."

This time the man looked him in the eye, actually looked at James with one eye, as the other eye was milky white. "Didn't you just jump ship, boy?" asked the African.

James could only nod. More waves slapped his face.

The black man looked toward Sullivan's Island, the quarantine area for all slavers entering Charles Town harbor. He shook his head. "Your ship might send a longboat to fetch us, and though I don't know what might come of you, I'd end up dead, or worse, back on the auction block."

Coughing saltwater, James gasped, "I was forced to jump ship."

"Why's that?"

"I helped . . . a black man . . . like you."

"Swear?" The African sat up. "Swear on your mother's grave?"

"Swear!" James coughed up more saltwater.

The black man regarded him. "Your mother really dead?"

Again, James could only nod. His arms were *sooo* tired and the waves would not let him be.

Before he knew what was happening, the old man had laid down his pole and grabbed him by his belt, pulling him over the side and into the skiff. Sprawling in the bottom, head and shoulders against the far side, James looked up to see his angel sail by. Actually, there were two of them on a passenger ship heading for Charles Town.

The old man dipped his oars into the water and shifted the smaller craft around to take the larger ship's wake at the oblique. As the larger ship passed, James saw that both angels had coal-black hair, bright blue eyes, and skin as white as porcelain. The younger of the two spotted James, flashed a huge smile, and waved. James tried to lift his arm to wave back, but as he did, the older girl gripped the younger girl's arm and guided her away from the railing.

Once the skiff broke through the wash, the old man grinned. "What you should do, boy, is find some way of laying claim to one of those girls. They're about the same age as you, and if they aren't spoken for, you just might have a chance."

James barely had the energy to shake his head. "Not me. I don't have a farthing to my name." He looked to where his former ship approached Sullivan's Island. "I didn't collect my wages before abandoning ship."

"Well," said the old man, "the way you came off that rigging, maybe you should sign on with one of those privateers headed for the Spanish Main. You might come back a rich man like Sir Henry Morgan." The African tapped his boat and laughed. "Maybe you'll return with a ship of your own."

FIVE

During the Golden Age of Piracy, South Carolina had more problems on its hands than just pirates. The Lords Proprietors, or those who owned the colony, repeatedly clashed with the Goose Creek men, a cagey group of political operatives who took their name from the area where many of them owned plantations. The Goose Creek men remained a burr under the Lords Proprietors' saddle, causing one governor after another to fall into their legislative traps. And members of various Indian nations, feeling cheated by traders or having their land encroached on—actions encouraged by the colonial government—members of those tribes would appear out of nowhere and slaughter isolated farming families, sending the survivors scurrying into Charles Town. The Yamassee War (1715–1718) so unnerved the colonists by the viciousness of the attacks that South Carolina mobilized every black and white man, slave, free, or indentured, to drive the Yamassee back across the Savannah River.

THE PIRATE AND THE BELLE

In London, the Lords Proprietors believed the Indian threat had ended with the defeat of the Yamassee. It was left to the governor to form an alliance with the Cherokees if the colony wanted to survive. Finally, with the Cherokees occupying the attention of the Lower Creeks and their allies, the colonists had a chance to catch their breath.

Then came the pirates.

Ever since Elizabeth I had been elevated to queen and found her treasury empty, the Crown had accumulated wealth through the use of bloodthirsty and strong-willed persons called "merchant adventurers." Unless one of those adventurers held out on the Crown, as Captain Kidd had done and paid with his life, anyone was free to make a living by ship and sword. In contrast, halfway around the world, China had pulled in its horns after decades of exploration; the emperor of China considered seafaring a terrible waste of resources. A similar inclination toward adventure and investigation was stopped cold in the Middle East when science collided with religion. This meant if there was to be any colonization, conquering, or missionary work done, it would have to be done by the squabbling nations of Europe.

In England, privateering was an honorable profession going all the way back to the days of John Hawkins and his cousin, Sir Francis Drake, both old seadogs working to break the stranglehold that Spain had on the Caribbean Basin, commonly known as the Spanish Main.

Years earlier, Portugal and Spain had taken their dispute over the New World to the Pope, and, as a result, a line had been drawn, divvying up the properties of the New World. In a giveaway that rivaled the purchase of Manhattan for twenty-four dollars' worth of cloth and buttons, the Portuguese claimed Brazil and kept their lucrative trade routes to India. Spain received everything else. That meant the Spanish controlled all the gold and silver mines in America, if, that is, they could safely ship all that gold and silver back to Spain.

So, for more than two hundred years, the annual convoy gathered off Havana and sailed for Spain, hundreds of ships filled with gold, silver, emeralds, and pearls. It was just too good a target to pass up, and for that reason, Drake and Hawkins had special ships built to pick off the weaker members of the pack. Sir Henry Morgan refined this process because of a loophole in the letter of marque that said privateers in service to the Crown did not have to share their spoils if such spoils were seized in a land battle.

For this reason, Sir Henry moored his ships down the coast and marched overland, sacking one Spanish city after another. In this way, he and his fellow buccaneers kept all the plunder, and before this window of opportunity closed, Morgan had invested in several sugar plantations, married a highborn lady, and cultivated a friendship with the governor of Jamaica. Born into a Welsh family of farmers, Sir Henry died not only a nobleman, but a very rich man.

Eventually, the mines played out, and Spain opened its ports in the New World to other countries. In return, England closed her ports to buccaneers. Overnight, thousands of licensed privateers were thrown out of work. Many of them turned to piracy.

SIX

Philip Morton was one of those pirates and Morton was the cannon master for the *Queen Anne's Revenge,* Blackbeard's flagship. While Blackbeard held Charles Town hostage, along with a good number of prominent citizens seized on ships entering or leaving the harbor, Morton and his minions strutted around Charles Town as if they owned the place. During Morton's strut, the cannon master spied a gorgeous young woman and dismissed his fellow pirates so to spend the remainder of the day following this young woman and her brother from one shop to another, that is, until the brother threatened to call on the good people of Charles Town to throw the pirate into the harbor.

Before that could happen, the brother spied a girl *he* had never had the courage to approach. Seizing his sister's arm, he pulled her into a millinery shop on Broad where she introduced him to the girl. While her brother stammered, and otherwise tried to hold a conversation, Marie Belle stepped back onto Broad where Philip Morton lay in wait. And though the pair moved no farther than a couple of feet from the door, Marie soon fell under the cannon master's spell, Morton filling the girl's head with images of what it was like to be a pirate, especially when he spoke of a pirate's ability to come and go as he, or she, pleased.

Piracy was not some fancy on Marie's part. She knew of one such Carolina girl, Anne Bonny, who had left home when her father refused to acknowledge her marriage to a small-time pirate, James Bonny. Anne and James ran off to the Bahamas and New Providence, an island well situated for budding pirates. New Providence was near all the major shipping lanes and was protected by currents, shoals, and surfs that made it near impossible for the Spanish to take action against.

On New Providence, James Bonny became an informant for the governor; Anne spent most of her time in taverns and took up with "Calico Jack" Rackham. Together, Anne and Jack stole a sloop, rounded up a crew, and took up a life of piracy. Together, Anne and Jack seized several ships and shared the spoils with their crew. That was their downfall. When attacked by a pirate hunter, Rackham's crew was too drunk to resist, but Anne fought like a tigress. And when Jack was allowed to visit Anne in her prison cell only days before he was to be hanged, Anne was reported to have said: "If you had fought like a man, Jack, you need not be hanged like a dog."

Because Anne was pregnant, she was given a stay of execution, and while completing her pregnancy, she disappeared from the Bahamas and reappeared in South Carolina. There, as legend tells us, Anne married again, had eight children, and died a respectable woman at the ripe old age of eighty-four.

Marie Belle was not actually a Belle, but an orphan who had attached herself to Antoine and Denis Belle while the father and son were traveling by way of the underground railroad from their native France to Switzerland. In Zurich, Marie's grandparents had pleaded with Antoine to take the child with him, that poor health made it impossible for the grandparents to continue. They said the girl's family had been murdered by one of the many mobs that appeared out of nowhere in Paris, and not always at the behest of the government. It would take France over a century to recover from the loss of these Huguenots, as these particular Protestants ran the country—and lorded over its Catholic masses.

So, the orphan Marie Torquet became Marie Belle, and Uncle Antoine cheered her up by inventing a new identity. Antoine even had the girl sit on his lap and recite Belle family history, chapter and verse, and over a period of time, Marie came to believe she had fallen in with a family that would share their largess once they reached Carolina.

Catherine dashed all those hopes once she and her sister arrived in Charles Town. She convinced Uncle Antoine to send Marie to Cooper Hill to live with François Belle, a distant relative and a much poorer one, where François, his three sons, and several Africans were busily diking land for the family's rice plantation. At

Cooper Hill, nature would take its course. After all, three strapping young men resided at Cooper Hill, and Marie was a winsome young lady.

As were Sparta and Athens centuries before, Charles Town had developed into a city-state continually under siege by the Spanish, French, and various Indian tribes. With more than a hundred private residences and quite a few businesses along the harbor, the colonists had built a brick wall around the city with several star-shaped bastions reinforced by cannons at crucial points, and a single entry point, a drawbridge where Broad met Meeting Street.

Still, by the end of Blackbeard's blockade, the brick wall was coming down and Charles Town was spilling into the countryside. As a further sign of sophistication, cattle, horses, and sheep were no longer allowed to run free, and the streets were regularly cleared of horse droppings. This former city-state was about to grow as no other in North America, leaving Boston, New York, and Philadelphia in its wake.

Catherine's sister, Nelie, wanted to be part of that growth, and the man she pined for owned a bridge, or wharf, across the street from her Uncle Antoine' shop. The wags at Belle Mercantile warned customers: Don't let yourself get caught between James Stuart and Nelie Belle whenever the former pirate enters the store. You just might be run down by the girl. The proposal by James Stuart for Nelie's hand in marriage was the final insult, and Catherine shipped her little sister off to live with relatives at Cooper Hill.

THE PIRATE AND THE BELLE

At Cooper Hill, François was busy creating what he called the Belle ancestral home, insisting that Cooper Hill would become the dominant rice plantation in the Low Country. Such a statement was almost laughable. In its current state Cooper Hill was nothing more than a muddy farm sporting a large cabin overlooking the river. There, Marie was expected to clean the cabin, cook the meals, wash and mend the clothing, and keep an eye on François's rice experiments. Like many other planters, François believed the Belles would lead the life of country gentry if he could only come up with the perfect strain of rice; as at the moment, the only money coming in was from the indigo planted on the high ground above the new rice fields.

It wasn't just the chores driving Marie mad, but the foregone conclusion that she would eventually marry one of François' sons and be stuck at Cooper Hill forever. Fueling Marie's rage were her occasional trips into Charles Town where she saw the clothing "cousin" Catherine wore, the family's manor house on Meeting Street, not to mention the number of handsome gentlemen immigrating to Carolina. If she could not live in Charles Town, then she would never live at Cooper Hill.

Marie's restlessness did not go overlooked, and for that reason, she was always accompanied by one of her "brothers" whenever she visited Charles Town, and when her "brother" dallied behind to speak to a young woman in a millinery shop, Marie was free at last. She could speak to anyone she chose, and Marie chose

Philip Morton because Blackbeard's cannon master could give her specific instructions as to how to escape the dreariness of Cooper Hill.

All it would take would be a late evening walk along the river where Morton would be waiting in a boat, and Morton cautioned Marie against bringing along more than what her purse might hold; no baggage or luggage, otherwise her family might become suspicious. Unfortunately for Marie, it was Nelie who took those lonely walks along the river while Marie was chastised by her surrogate father.

"Because of your latest trip to Charles Town, you are far behind with your chores," said François. "There will be no walks along the river for the next few nights."

SEVEN

Leaving a mule-drawn cart parked in the street, Samuel Chase rang the bell at the outside door of James Stuart's single house, and Chase, the quartermaster for the *Mary Stewart*, didn't stop pulling the cord until Julia opened the door. The maid stepped back, one hand reaching through a slit in her dress.

Chase ignored the pistol, stepped across the piazza, and entered the house. The stairs he took two at a time, and since he'd put in some time building the place, he knew his way around. A tall, broad-shouldered man, Chase was one of the few former privateers who still wore a beard cut in the style of Sir Francis Drake, one of Chase's heroes. His reddish-blond hair was pulled back into a pigtail.

In the master bedroom, he found Stuart drinking coffee and shaving at a mirror hanging over a washstand. The porcelain shaving bowl sat in a hole cut into the top of the washstand. Chase saw Stuart look at him in the convex surface of the mirror. The

Scot wore no shirt, exposing a chest matted with hair. Stuart was built more compactly than Chase, with larger arms, the better to swing a broadsword. Where Chase was a premier organizer and planner, James Stuart was a natural born leader, always at the head of any boarding party, swinging his broadsword and clearing a path for those who followed.

"I've had a broadside plastered to the wall of every tavern, ordinary, and coffeehouse, notifying the crew that the *Mary Stewart* sails with the tide," said Chase. "That should bring in the old hands and quite a few others, if they're not in jail or the stocks. The ship's surgeon has agreed to collect the signatures dockside and read the articles of agreement to the illiterate."

Towel over his shoulder and straight razor in his hand, Stuart turned away from the mirror. "And why would you do that, laddie?"

"It's what you would've done if you hadn't been drunk the last week. Some of Blackbeard's men took a punt up the Cooper and snatched him a bride."

Stuart frowned. Nelie had been sent to Cooper Hill so she'd have no further contact with him. Maybe the Belle family thought he and Nelie would run off together . . . which wasn't such a bad idea. He, himself, owned more than one ship.

Chase saw he wasn't getting through. "Captain, the story is that one of the girls at Cooper Hill was kidnapped, the other hanged herself. The dead girl is Marie Belle."

The straight razor fell from Stuart's hand and hit the floor. Stuart was wiping shaving cream from his face as he crossed the room. "Blackbeard took Nelie?"

"According to those who saw Marie Belle speaking to a pirate in front of millinery shop on Broad, it was Philip Morton or one of his agents."

At the bedroom door, Stuart dropped the towel and snatched down a shirt from a wooden peg. He also brought along a leather vest and strapped on the sheathed dagger he was never without. "What were Teach's men doing in Charles Town?"

"You have been drunk too long."

Buttoning his shirt going out the bedroom door, Stuart flashed Chase a sharp look. "I wasn't drunk long enough to forget that I was denied the woman I love and that you're running the bridge for a percentage of all goods passing through, so why was it all that important I remain sober?" He tossed his jacket over his shoulder for his quartermaster to catch. "I ask again: What was Blackbeard doing in Charles Town?"

"Blockading the harbor for a chest of medicine."

Stuart stopped at the head of the stairs. "Medicine? What the devil did Teach want with medicine?"

"Oh, he took what he wanted from ships exiting and entering the harbor—he had at least five ships in his fleet—but upon the pain of death of the passengers, he wouldn't leave Charles Town without that chest of medicine."

Stuart tucked in his shirt as they descended the stairs. "Have you employed anyone to track his movements?"

"Once the blockade was lifted, I put teams on ships sailing for Philadelphia, the Outer Banks, and the Main. If they sight Teach, one of them will return to Charles Town, the other will follow Blackbeard."

At the door of the piazza stood a huge African wearing a pair of breeches and a leather vest. His hair was woven into locks, his skin bore many scars, and his arms were covered with tattoos.

"Is it true, Captain?" asked the black man, whose name was Alexander. "I'm to be given another chance to kill Blackbeard?"

Stuart took his jacket from Chase. "If Samuel has his facts straight."

The black man looked at the quartermaster.

Chase nodded.

The African grinned, then clapped his hands together and rubbed them for good measure. "Oh, this *is* good news. Blackbeard will never surrender. He will fight to the death." Alexander had once been marooned by Blackbeard over a difference of opinion in the employment of cannon in the attack. Rescued by James Stuart, it wasn't long before the African had earned the position of cannon master on Stuart's flagship, the *Mary Stewart*.

The black man followed the two white men through the front door and down the steps where the mule-drawn cart waited. Up and down the street, traffic moved briskly, though there were those who cursed the mule and cart in their way.

"Most of the cannoneers will be drunk," explained Alexander, following Chase into the cart. "We'll join you at the ship, Captain."

Behind them, Julia opened the door, came down the steps, and handed a basket to Alexander. When Alexander tried to pull back the checkered cloth and look inside, Julia slapped his hand.

"For the captain, fool!"

Alexander jerked his hand back. He appeared wounded.

"Captain," asked the maid, "will you want your sea chest sent down to the harbor?"

"Of course," said Stuart, smiling. "What would I do without you, Julia?"

"Probably marry some white woman to lord over me." The maid turned to go. "Send a hand in an hour or so."

"Er—Julia, what about that little brunette I almost wed?"

From the door, the black woman faced him. "Don't matter what color their hair—all white women are bossy." And after a long look at Alexander, she disappeared into the house.

"That's the pot calling the kettle black," muttered the African, huddled on the seat in the cart.

Chase slapped the African on the back. "Looks like Alexander has a new girlfriend."

The cannon master said nothing, only clutched the basket and stared down Meeting Street.

"You could do worse."

Chase shook the reins, and the cart began negotiating its way through the oncoming traffic. Stuart followed them down the cobblestone street in the direction of Broad.

Approaching from the opposite direction was the colonial governor. "Oh, I see," said Johnson from his buggy. "When they kidnap your fiancée you stoop to defend the honor of Charles Town."

Johnson rose up in the buggy and shouted, probably

for the benefit of those on Meeting Street. "Drunk the entire time Blackbeard held this city hostage. You haven't heard the last of this, Captain Stuart. Charles Town will be talking about this long after they stopped wondering why I didn't hang you for piracy."

As he passed the governor's buggy, Stuart said, "Probably because you always received your percentage."

Stuart knew that only stupid pirates didn't share their booty, and those were the ones usually hanged. Still, as Stuart turned on Broad, he could not put the thought from his mind: Charles Town blockaded. Why hadn't someone told him?

But Stuart knew the answer. He'd been told, and on more than one occasion, that he was a very nasty drunk!

Evidently, Stuart hadn't heard the last of this, because, walking the length of Broad, an anxious young man, wearing workman's clothing, fell in beside him.

"Captain Stuart, I'm Rodney Wickham, and I hear you're hiring."

Stuart looked at the young man, especially his hands. "Are you an able-bodied seaman?"

"Well, no, sir, but—"

"Stuart & Company only hires experienced seamen."

"But you must hire me. My mother's been insulted."

Stuart glanced at Wickham. "By the clothing you wear, sir, it must not have been much of an insult. I recommend you let it be."

Wickham took Stuart's arm, stopping the Scot before he could cross Church Street.

Stuart glanced at the hand, his own hand on the sheathed dagger at his belt. "Unhand me, sir."

Wickham did not remove his hand, nor did the anxiety disappear from his face. "But—but he locked my mother in the hold, Blackbeard, that is. Said he'd kill her if he didn't receive the ransom."

Stuart removed Wickham's hand from his arm. "The insult to your mother and the other passengers will be avenged. The *Mary Stewart* sails with the tide. You just won't be on it."

Stuart crossed Church Street and continued toward the harbor where a dour looking man fell in step with him. The dour looking man wore a black suit.

"Good to see you up and about, Captain."

Now Stuart stopped—for the personal attorney of the Wragg family, and if anyone in Charles Town did not respect Samuel Wragg, Stuart had yet to meet the man. Wragg was not only rich, but a member of the royal council that set policy for the colony.

The attorney cleared his throat. "While you were indisposed, my client and his son came to believe they would never leave Blackbeard's ship alive. The boy, William, is only four and remains in a state of anxiety, from which, I doubt he'll ever recover.

"If you're not aware, the boat sent ashore with the representatives of the hostages was guarded by two of Blackbeard's shipmates. Unfortunately, a squall blew in, overturning the craft. Though all souls were saved, once the ransom, in this case a chest of medicine, was loaded for the return trip, the two pirates who had accompanied the passengers ashore were nowhere to be found."

"Let me guess," said Stuart. "They were found drunk in some bordello."

"That they were, Captain Stuart, and during the extra two days, and well beyond the deadline set by Blackbeard, young William and his father thought their lives forfeit because of the delay. It was only because of my client's powers of persuasion that none of the hostages came to harm."

"And what would Mr. Wragg have me do?"

"Well, sir," said the dour looking man, "since you now find yourself in a similar position, we do have a suggestion."

EIGHT

At Stuart's Bridge, or wharf, the *Mary Stewart* was flanked by other three-masted ships, their bowsprits reaching out as if attempting to touch the buildings on the other side of East Bay. The figurehead on the *Mary Stewart was* Mary Stuart, as well as Stuart remembered his mother, and because France and England spent so much time at war, the ship did not bear the French spelling of his surname. Stuart had been given the ship by his former captain, Benjamin Hornigold, just as Hornigold had given Blackbeard his first ship, a French slaver renamed the *Queen Anne's Revenge.*

You could purchase anything you wanted along East Bay: food, clothing, furniture; any manufactured goods available in Europe. The buildings were two and three stories tall, many with residences on the second and third floors. Jammed cheek by jowl, East Bay was the center of commerce for the Carolinas; North Carolina having few decent harbors.

Stuart crossed the street to the screeches of gulls searching for their next meal, the lapping of the Cooper against the harbor wall, and the groan of rope from ships moored at various wharfs. Halfway across East Bay, a black man intercepted him.

"Begging your pardon," said Caesar, doffing his hat, "but my master would like to have a word with you."

"I'm really not interested in anything the Belles have to say."

The black man chased after him, dodging traffic, and there was a good bit of it: wagons, men on horseback, men without horses, ladies in buggies, and carts with fresh produce from farms on the Neck.

"Captain, please, it's about Miss Nelie. You've heard she's been taken by Blackbeard."

Stuart stopped at the edge of the bridge. Streaming past him were members of the crew headed for the ship's surgeon standing behind a lectern at the foot of the gangway. The surgeon was collecting signatures for the articles of agreement.

Stuart winced at the sight of the lectern. Now, where had that come from? Opposite the *Mary Stewart* was the warehouse for Stuart & Company and the long and narrow building dominated the bridge.

The black man gestured at a carriage across the street. "Mr. Belle would like to invite you for a cup of tea before the *Mary Stewart* weighs anchor."

"Caesar, I have a ship to rig." Seeing the disappointed look on the servant's face, he added, "But I'll stop by before we sail. I simply don't know when that will be."

Caesar smiled and returned his hat to his head. "Yes, sir, I'll tell him you'll be along shortly."

At eight bells, or the conclusion of the afternoon watch, Stuart climbed down to the main deck and noticed Denis Belle standing on the wharf, leaning on a cane.

Stuart nodded to the Frenchman, who returned the nod. Stuart knew there would be some pleading and whining, perhaps even an offer of money. He would turn everything down. Nelie was the best of the lot, and, in truth, no family was haughtier than the Belles of Charles Town, something about originally being from Paris. Run out of Paris, truth be known.

Before Stuart could join Belle, a man in a black suit and tricorn hat intercepted him with a quill, ink bottle, and a sheet of paper. "I've checked below, and I believe your ship can hold up to one hundred kegs of either whiskey or rum."

"Make it fifty of each and have it onboard before nightfall."

Stuart dipped the quill in the ink and signed the paperwork. Joining them was a stout man, the ship's boatswain, Fitzsimmons.

Looking up from the paperwork, Stuart said, "Fitzsimmons, it'll be your job to secure it." Stuart gestured at a board fastened to the railing at the head of the gangway. Written on it in chalk was the next high tide. "That's how much time you have."

The merchant hesitated, and it had little to do with the next high tide. "Captain Stuart, this is a considerable order."

The Scot only stared at him.

"Well," said the man, clearing his throat, "some collateral would be helpful. You are going in harm's way."

Stuart told him to see Samuel Wragg's attorney. At the sound of Wragg's name, the merchant brightened and disappeared down the gangway.

Hearing lines creak overhead, Stuart looked up. The crew had begun the arduous process of unloading the cargo to the screams and curses of the senior sailors. Empty nets were lowered into the hold, where they were filled, and then the heavy nets made their return trip to the warehouse on the wharf. Despite complaints about the rush to sail with the next high tide, the crew was thrilled to be free of polishing brass, repairing rigging, and patching sails. They were going pirate hunting!

Fitzsimmons followed Stuart to the head of the gangway. "I'll be needing a bit of wood, Captain."

Stuart gestured at Denis Belle on the bridge below. "See him. I hear the Belles just bought a sawmill."

"Aye, aye, sir." And down the gangway went Fitzsimmons.

After Stuart informed several hands coming up the gangway that he was in the market for seamen who could not only load but defend a ship's cargo, he joined Belle on the wharf. On his way down the gangway, Stuart passed men missing fingers, limbs, and eyes; the men's skin was covered with tattoos and their flesh burnt nearly black from long hours in the sun. Scrapes, bruises, and black eyes were from the last few days ashore and worn as badges of honor.

When the Frenchman straightened up from his cane, Stuart asked. "What can I do for you, Mr. Belle?"

Denis Belle spoke English with a decidedly French accent. "I was afraid you would not take my invitation seriously."

THE PIRATE AND THE BELLE

Belle wore a coat, waistcoat, and knee britches, silk stockings and shoes fastened with large silver buckles. The coat was collarless, knee length, with cuffs that turned back to the elbow, exposing the lace trim of the shirt beneath. The stockings came up over the edges of the knee britches, held up by a beribboned garter. His cape was short and weighted, this for street fighting, and his tricorn hat had wiring to protect his head from blows.

"I doubt I'll have time for tea, but we can talk over here." Stuart gestured toward East Bay, and the two men moved away from the line of sailors. "Fitzsimmons spoke to you about the additional lumber?" asked Stuart.

Belle gestured with his cane toward Belle Mercantile across the street. "I referred him to Mr. Huger. The lumber will be here within the hour."

The two men stopped at the end of the warehouse. "Actually, Captain Stuart, it's not your word that concerns me, but the vulgar display made by my wife earlier today. It might put you off having anything to do with the Belle family."

"The thought had crossed my mind, but if you've come to apologize, don't. As men we know there's little to be gained by trying to understand women. I hold no grudge against your wife or any other member of your family."

"Then I will await you in the cool of my father's shop." With a wan smile, Denis added, "You may find there is a good bit of money involved in my proposition." And touching his hat, Belle held up his cane and slowed the traffic on East Bay.

Stuart watched him go. How that man, or any man, could remain married to Catherine Belle was a mystery to him.

Part of the traffic was a mule-drawn cart, and when the cart turned onto the bridge, Samuel Chase hopped off, but Alexander continued down the bridge, shouting at the sailors to make way. The rear of the cart was filled with sailors, most lying on their backs, several moaning, and all shading their eyes from the afternoon sun.

When the cart reached the gangway, the cannon master ordered the surgeon to move the lectern to where the bridge met East Bay. Former crewmates passed Stuart and Chase, some headed for the gangway, others headed in the opposite direction.

"You'll have to offer more than that to get me to sail against Blackbeard," said one of the departing seamen.

His companion nodded in agreement as they left the bridge.

Chase was watching Belle disappear into his father's store. "Did they offer compensation?" he asked.

"No, but they will. Samuel, see that the ship is properly lightened. There's many a sandbar where we are headed."

Chase returned his attention to Stuart. "You think Blackbeard's headed for the Outer Banks?"

"Well, it's that time of year when Teach does his pirating in the North Atlantic."

"And how many ships shall we man?"

"We have two others in port and shall take them both, though I may have to find someone to captain one of them. In that case, that captain would be you and Ward will be dismissed. Also, you should know that there are one hundred kegs of whiskey and rum to be delivered before nightfall, so you'd better have more than one abstainer on guard."

Chase couldn't believe what he was hearing. "You think Teach will trade liquor for Nelie?"

"Teach has almost five hundred men under his command, so going in cannons blazing isn't in the best interest of Miss Belle."

It took a moment for the quartermaster to regain his bearings. This was a side of Stuart that Chase had never seen. The Belle woman had really gotten to him. "Captain, you do understand that if this was anyone but Nelie, I wouldn't be sailing with you."

"Samuel, I'm pleased that you invested in that bakery, but I cannot see you as a baker."

"There's no better baker in Carolina than my Susannah, and it will stop some of the talk."

Stuart didn't know what Chase meant and said so.

"It'll be difficult for people to consider me a wild-eyed pirate if they see me wearing an apron and covered with flour."

Now Stuart understood. One of the first things the privateers had to learn when they came ashore was to shave their beards, cover their tattoos, and, stranger yet, lose their sun-baked tans. In truth, when they first arrived, few people could detect a difference between Alexander and the two white men.

The ship's surgeon nodded at them as he set up the lectern near East Bay. He appeared tipsy, and this caused Stuart to glance in the direction of the *Mary Stewart.*

Alexander was cursing the sailors on the rear of the cart and kicking them off when they didn't move fast enough. It took a few minutes, but finally the cannoneers staggered down the bridge to the lectern and fell into line to hear the surgeon read the articles of agreement. Behind them, sailors moved up and down the gangway with items from the warehouse, items not moved in bulk by the nets, such as extra flints and patch material for pistols and muskets.

"Doctor," asked Stuart, "would you have any idea where that lectern came from?"

The surgeon held onto the lectern and leaned back as if to see it better. "St. Philip's, I do believe."

Stuart only shook his head. Stealing from the Church of England . . . When would people ever learn?

Chase noticed Stuart's concern. "I'll make sure it's returned, Captain. It's on the way to the bakery, and I wasn't going to leave without a basket of my wife's sticky buns. With Susannah's indenture finished, it's time to settle down and have those children we've always talked about. I didn't tell you, but one's on the way, perhaps two, the way Susannah's put on weight."

Stuart offered the man his hand. Like Chase's, it was firm and rough from days of handling lines. "I didn't know. Congratulations, Samuel."

Releasing Stuart's grasp, Chase clapped the Scot on the shoulder. "And we'll find Nelie. Don't you worry."

Stuart nodded as he watched members of the crew sign the articles of agreement. "Samuel, a good number of veteran sailors have signed on, but Queen Anne's War is well behind us, and we don't need anyone who's become fat, dumb, and sassy since they last tried to board a sloop in the face of cannon fire." He pointed at the lectern. "Make sure they understand there will be no vote on our destination or negotiating of the spoils. Everything will be . . ."

Stuart's voice trailed off at the sound of clanking chains around the wrists and ankles of a large white man with a pink face, white beard, and wearing a stocking cap. The size of the prisoner had been enough to stop traffic when he shambled across East Bay. He was guarded by a small man with a musket.

The constable jerked his thumb at the man in chains. "The Irishman says if we let him out of the stocks you'll take him along and Charles Town will be rid of him. That's what the provost marshal sent me here to learn, Captain Stuart."

Chase said they would take him, but Stuart asked, "What was Kyrle in the stocks for?"

"Well, he pretty much tore up that tavern on the old Indian path out on the Neck."

"Captain," pleaded Kyrle, "I didn't have much choice. Those farmers called me a liar, saying I didn't sail with Sir Henry."

The constable shook his head. "If every pirate I knew sailed with Morgan . . ." When Kyrle glared at him, the constable stepped back, lowered his musket, and pointed it at the Irishman's rather large stomach. "Watch it, Kyrle. I ain't taking no prisoners."

Stuart asked, "So, how many of Kyrle's opponents had to be tended to after the fracas ended?"

"Five." The constable thought for a moment. "There might've been a sixth, but he made it away under his own steam."

"Then we'll take him," said Stuart.

Kyrle turned to the smaller man and held out his hands.

The constable shook his head. "No chance of that." He fished a key from his breeches and handed it to the huge man. "Just drop the key and chains on the street and get on the ship, Kyrle."

As the Irishman freed himself, he said, "Captain, I know where there are four more like me if you'll have them."

"If you mean sailors able to climb rigging and fight, even under cannon fire, we'll take them."

"Yes, sir, and that's what you'll have." On his fingers, Kyrle ticked off the names, then looked at the constable. "That is, if this little fellow will allow me the run of the waterfront for the next hour or so."

"That'll be the day."

"I'll vouch for him."

Behind Stuart, a line had formed at the lectern. Rodney Wickham was in that line, his face hidden by a broad-brimmed, felt hat.

"I don't know," said the constable, shaking his head.

Stuart asked, "What if I gave you an eight if Kyrle returns with those four men or ones equal to them?" Spain had flooded the world with so much silver that pieces of eight had created the first universal market, stretching from Spain all the way around the world.

"Real silver?" asked the constable.

"You can try to take a bite out of it if you like."

The two men shook on it, and the constable placed his musket on his shoulder and gathered up the chains. "Well, Mr. Kyrle, it appears you and I have some business to attend to."

Chase was staring at the cargo being netted from the ship's hold to the warehouse on Stuart's Bridge. Holding forth on the main deck, Alexander cursed and shouted that he'd better see their best effort, every man jack of them, or they'd never sail with Stuart & Company again.

"Some good should come from all this. There'll be plenty of upset customers." Chase realized what he'd said. "Sorry, Captain."

"Apology accepted. When we return, I intend to make Nelie my wife—despite the objections of her family."

Chase understood. He was trying to make a marriage work with a woman whose family still considered him a pirate, and in his case, it wasn't Susannah's immediate family objecting—all her family had died of cholera in London—but the family Susannah had been indentured to.

"Still, I hope the Belles offer a sizeable reward . . ."

"Well," said Stuart, starting across East Bay, "that's probably why they want to parley."

NINE

Very few people knew the real story of why Denis Belle and his father, Antoine, had immigrated to the New World. True, both were Huguenots and their family had been persecuted in their native land, but their motivation ran much deeper. Denis, having been ambushed by three men in what turned out to be a phony duel, killed two of the men with his sword, and with help from his father, seriously wounded the other.

When Antoine Belle realized there would be no justice for his son in Paris, as all three victims were Catholics, they quit France, leaving behind their property and two older sisters who had married into devout Catholic families. Denis's mother had banknotes sewn into her petticoats, but at the last minute said she couldn't give up her grandchildren. Instead, she gave up her petticoats, joined a nunnery, and converted to Catholicism.

So, via an underground railroad to Switzerland,

father and son followed other Calvinists to London and the Carolina Coffee Shop on Birchin Lane where a member of the Lords Proprietors held court every Tuesday and touted the virtues of immigrating to the colony of Carolina. Still, Antoine and Denis could not have been more surprised when they and the girl, Marie Torquet, found Charles Town to be nothing more than a frontier town, much of it surrounded by a brick wall and unmatched forests outside that wall. With money from his wife's petticoats, Antoine built a house on Meeting Street, one appropriate for a Parisian gentleman, and then, he, his son, and the girl awaited the verdict of the first "sickly season."

It was believed that if a colonist could survive the first round of illnesses, they would be "seasoned" and had a better chance to survive further sickly seasons, which arrived each summer, regular as clockwork. But what the colonists had to survive were not only diseases native to the New World. Europeans had brought with them smallpox, malaria, yellow fever, and typhus, and never once questioned why the natives refused to live along the coast. Lured by the near tropical climate, immigrants came to Carolina and died by the hundreds. Once the Belles survived their first sickly season, though it had been touch-and-go for Marie, Antoine looked for a place to invest his remaining money.

He purchased a piece of property along the Cooper River where a distant relative and his three sons were put to work turning Cooper Hill into a rice plantation. The distant relative's wife had not survived the first sickly season, and their family had arrived in Carolina virtually penniless. Still, it would be years before

Cooper Hill turned a pound, so Antoine invested in a bankrupt mercantile store on East Bay. Clerks were hired, merchandise dusted off, and new merchandise purchased. From there, everything went downhill fast with two gentlemen trying to run a store without getting their hands dirty. When Catherine and Nelie arrived, Catherine realized something needed to be done, and quickly. Cooper Hill and Belle Mercantile were eating into the family's resources.

Catherine proposed marriage to her cousin, Denis, and that she be allowed a free hand in running the store. Observing that there was no manufacturing in a town with a thriving harbor, it wasn't long before Catherine replaced many of the goods in Belle Mercantile from a factory she had built outside the wall on Charles Town Neck. The factory began turning out goods used by ships, and importing rope. Belle Mercantile sold a great deal of rope, and with this factory, Catherine learned the value of good proxy. Actually, she went through several men before entrusting the factory to a vulgar and profane Welshman who could certainly turn out the work, but made Catherine so uneasy with his language that she found herself attending services every time the French church opened its doors.

As for Denis Belle, he had never met anyone like his cousin, and in truth, had paid her scant attention in Paris. Catherine was always the little girl sitting in the corner, minding her little sister, but mostly watching everyone, watching everything. Almost ten years older, Denis became fascinated with the organizational abilities of his new wife, that is, as long as someone could keep Catherine's mouth shut. Catherine was all business, all the time, and Denis and his father were above that. They had emigrated from France to Carolina to become landed gentry, not merchant princes.

And it was into this world, through the doors of Belle Mercantile and an office in the rear of the store, that a clerk ushered James Stuart. There, he found Denis Belle sitting behind a desk, his wife in a chair off to one side, and a clerk duplicating purchase orders and invoices that would later be stored in a safe at the Belle home on Meeting Street. This gave Stuart pause. Fires were an ever-present danger. Perhaps he could learn a thing or two from these Frenchies.

Catherine cleared her throat, and her husband asked the clerk if he could find something to do in the front of the store. Nodding, the clerk put down his quill, stoppered his ink, and left the room, closing the door behind him.

Now Denis cleared *his* throat. "Captain Stuart, we would like to discuss your proposal of marriage to my sister-in-law."

"Oh," said Stuart, laughing, "I'm good enough for Nelie now that she's damaged goods."

At this remark, Catherine colored and shifted around in her chair, but Stuart did not see this. His attention was focused on her husband. What women had to say in such matters was irrelevant.

"Captain Stuart, that is no way to speak of a lady."

"Sir, if you believed Nelie was still a lady, you would've come out from behind that desk and tried to land a blow on me."

Catherine Belle *was* on her feet, stepping across the

room and slapping Stuart with a blow that turned the Scotsman's head. She said: "I will not have you speak of my sister in that manner. You, sir, forget to whom you are speaking."

Stuart looked at the woman. "Mrs. Belle, what is it you want of me? I have a ship to rig."

"First," said Catherine, face still flushed, "you will apologize for what you insinuated about my sister."

Stuart stared at her for the longest, then he apologized. After all, it was in *his* best interest if Nelie were considered chaste.

"Very well," said Catherine, returning to her seat. "I accept your apology. Just don't let it happen again."

Catherine returned her attention to her husband, which was enough to prompt Denis to relate the tale about Nelie being mistaken for Marie and kidnapped from Cooper Hill.

Stuart cut him off. "I know the story."

"Very well," said Denis. "A Huguenot pastor awaits the return of the *Mary Stewart* and will attend to your marriage."

Catherine fidgeted in her chair. "What fool would name his flagship after a Papist, I cannot fathom! They have a whole colony for Papists in Maryland. You Catholics should all settle there."

"Catherine," began Denis, "please don't speak so irrationally. If Captain Stuart were a—"

Again Stuart cut him off. "Mrs. Belle, you need to watch of whom *you* are speaking. My mother is dead, and both of us were members of the Kirk of Scotland."

Catherine waved this off, apparently unable to grasp

anything said by the Scot. "The pastor knows of the engagement of which my husband and our uncle agreed more than a week ago. The necessary announcement was made yesterday morning at both services. We shall not wait for Twelfth Night."

Stuart canted his head. "You're pretty sure of yourself, lady."

"Captain Stuart," said Denis Belle, "I think what my wife is trying to say is that there will be a substantial dowry."

"For taking Nelie off your hands."

Again Catherine was out of her chair and swinging at Stuart. This time he caught her hand, then her other hand when it came swinging his way. Kicked in the shin, Stuart pushed the woman away and into the arms of her husband, who had finally come around the desk. Catherine's face remained flush when she was reseated in her chair and restrained by her husband.

"You pirates . . . you pirates . . ." she said, then, just as suddenly, her shoulders slumped and she began to weep.

"Privateer, Mrs. Belle, in service to the Crown."

Her husband furnished a handkerchief to his wife, but remained between his wife and the former privateer. "Captain Stuart, will you do this for us? Will you find my sister-in-law and return her to Charles Town?"

"Oh, he'll do it," said Catherine from behind her husband's back. She straightened her shoulders and dabbed at her eyes with the handkerchief. "Show him the papers."

"Catherine," said Denis, glancing over his shoulder, "there's no cause for that."

"I'm not signing anything," said Stuart, heading for the door.

"Oh, Captain Stuart," said Catherine, with considerable sarcasm, "I'm very familiar with your method of conducting business. You are incapable of signing anything unless it puts you impossibly in debt and creates margins that are much too thin."

Still, before he opened the door, Stuart took pity on the woman. "Mrs. Belle, let me tell you how this will play out. I will find Nelie and return her home. What fool you marry her to is none of my concern."

"Captain Stuart, Nelie is to marry you." Denis hesitated, biting his lip. "That is, if she's alive. You must understand my sister-in-law knows nothing of . . ." Denis glanced at his wife. ". . . of my family's previous rejection of your marital offer."

Stuart could not believe what he was hearing. "You didn't tell Nelie that I'd proposed marriage." Opening the door, he added, "You Frenchies are crazy, and the less I have to do with you, the better."

As he left the office and headed toward the front of the building, he heard Catherine Belle shouting, "Show him the papers! Show him the papers!"

For the life of him, Stuart could not understand what papers the Belles had that would hold any interest for him, but halfway down the hallway Denis caught up with him, taking Stuart's arm. Stuart glanced at the hand, causing Denis Belle to release his hold.

"I meant no offense," said the Frenchman.

The Scot said he took none. Every man along the waterfront knew Denis Belle was henpecked. Still, he was one of the best shots with a pistol and excelled in the use of a rapier. Not a bad thing when other men considered you a fool. Such skills encouraged men to hold their tongues.

As they entered the public sector of the building, Denis asked, "Captain Stuart, would you join me for a drink?"

"I really don't have the time."

Denis gestured behind them. "But I must explain why my wife is so upset."

"I would imagine it has something to do with the possibility of losing the last surviving member of her immediate family. That happened to me, and I'm in complete sympathy with your wife. She should be upset. I know I was." Crossing the retail portion of the store, Stuart ran into the man who handled his financial affairs.

After exchanging the social amenities, the lawyer said, "I'm sorry, Captain Stuart, but there was little I could do." He appeared embarrassed, glancing at the floor when adding, "On land, one must play by a different set of rules." The attorney doffed his hat and hurried out the door.

Stuart stepped out on East Bay and watched the man go, actually drifting in the same direction. This made it possible for Denis Belle to take him by the arm and continue down the street to the Carolina Tavern. Inside, the tavern keeper, a jolly fellow, greeted them.

"Perhaps one of your chambers upstairs?" asked Belle.

The jolly man nodded, clapped Stuart on the shoulder, and led the two men upstairs to a small room holding a table and four chairs. Stuart had been in this room before, playing whist. It was a plain thing with only one window, no pictures, and the most ordinary furniture. Before Stuart could take a seat, the wife of the tavern owner placed a tray holding large mugs of rum in the center of the table and left. The tray also held a new deck of cards. The tavern owner smiled, bowed, and shut the door as he went out the door backwards.

Stuart may have been stunned into silence with the chance meeting of his attorney, but now he found his tongue. "What are these papers of which your wife spoke?"

Denis waved off Stuart's concern and leaned back in his chair, taking one of the mugs with him. "It's nothing. Catherine purchased the notes on your ships, bridge, and house."

Stuart had reached for the other mug. Now, he straightened up and forgot all about his drink. "What do you mean? A woman cannot own property, unless said property is held in trust for a minor."

After sipping from his mug, Denis said, "Quite correct. It's my name on the notes. They were sold to me by your attorney."

"But for what good reason?"

"To make sure you did as Catherine requested."

"But why should I be concerned as to what your wife desires?"

"Well," said Denis, smiling, "you really don't think I'm shrewd enough to conduct such business transactions, do you?"

Stuart blinked. Never before had he met a member of the gentry who raised the issue of his own limitations.

"Captain Stuart, you must understand that although we Belles have considerable resources, all that concerns my wife is how those resources may be used to raise our family's station in life. We shall not be returning to England once we have made our fortune, and even with money, we are not welcomed in France."

"And as I said before, Mr. Belle, I care nothing for that. Is it true that Nelie has no idea that your family rejected my proposal of marriage?"

"That is true." He glanced at the closed door. "Give me a moment to round up a Bible and I will swear on it."

"Then know this," said Stuart, getting to his feet on the other side of the table, "once I find your sister-in-law, if she will have me, I will sail the *Mary Stewart* to the Bahamas and make a life for us on New Providence. We will not be returning to Charles Town."

A pained look crossed the Frenchman's face. "Captain Stuart, I do wish you wouldn't make this any more difficult than it is."

"I'm sorry, Mr. Belle, but that's how it must be."

"Captain Stuart, you cannot sail anywhere unless you own a ship, and as for taking an unmarried woman to the Bahamas, well, how would that look?"

"But I do own a ship. More than one, and the bridge that bears my name, and I shall marry the girl."

"Of course you do, and as of yesterday, Belle Mercantile carries those mortgages and can redeem them at our pleasure, not to mention I don't think the governor would issue you a license to marry."

It wasn't marriage on the Scot's mind. "But how can that be, that you carry my mortgages?"

"It is the way of commerce, as your lawyer explained."

"Then I will sell the house on Meeting Street. There have been offers, and I'll have no need for it if I leave Charles Town. I'll sell it all, even at a loss, just to rid myself of your family."

"Captain Stuart, you will never be rid of the Belle family. Not only are you and Nelie to be married, but the two of you are expected for dinner after the morning service each Sunday. And if you doubt that your note may be called in, an action backed by the colonial government, I must point out, by the time you've rescued Nelie, which we all certainly hope you can do, Catherine will have you tied up in court and you'll never set foot again on the *Mary Stewart,* or any of your other ships. That would go for your bridge and your new home on Meeting Street."

Stuart opened his hands in dismay. "But—but this makes no sense. Lawyers don't operate that way."

"My wife does."

"But why do you allow her to do so?"

"Captain Stuart, since you and I are to become brothers-in-law, you must learn that Catherine is very clever. Belle Mercantile was practically bankrupt when she took over. And married me." Denis smiled. "Though I don't think marriage was her primary concern, but my surname is Belle, and once we have children, the family name will be carried on. That is why Catherine comes into the shop every day, and when the door to that office is closed, the office where we met only moments ago, Catherine sits behind that desk you saw me sitting behind."

Stuart didn't know what to make of this but figured it might be best to rejoin Belle at the table. He took a seat and drank deeply from his mug. "But a woman operating a business . . ."

"You thought she was nothing more than a quarrelsome old scold, didn't you?" Again Denis smiled. "Well, certainly not old."

Stuart leaned forward. The gravity of the situation had finally sunk in. "Your wife purchased the notes on my ship, the bridge, my house, everything?"

"Oh, it's more than that. Catherine purchased the note on your quartermaster's new bakery, and I must say Mrs. Chase is an excellent pastry cook. I should know. Our family comes from Paris where some of the best—"

"But how does she come by my notes?"

"Why, the same way anyone secures what they want in the world of commerce. She paid more than market value. Of course, she doesn't make such offers. That's my job. And because of my reputation as a foolish man with unlimited resources, I can take any proposition to any lawyer in Charles Town."

"But I still don't understand. What is it that your wife wants?"

"Why, Captain Stuart, only what every family wants: to make a place for our family in this New World."

TEN

But when Denis Belle arrived later that day with a sea chest, Stuart took one look at the chest Caesar bore on his shoulder and motioned the two men into his cabin.

Once the servant had been dismissed, Stuart asked, "Just what in the devil do you think you're doing, Mr. Belle?" From the other side of the cabin door came the sound of hammers and saws and the contradictory shouts of sailors.

Belle straightened his shoulders and tossed back his cape. At the Frenchman's waist was a sword, at the other side a sheathed dagger. "You know of my reputation as a duelist?"

"But there will be no duels where we're headed, not unless I have Blackbeard in my sights, and then I very much doubt Teach and I will cross swords."

"More of a reason for me to make the trip. Someone must keep in mind the safety of my sister-in-law."

Stuart's eyes narrowed. "I rather thought that would

be my responsibility." Actually, Stuart figured he would entrust Nelie into the good hands of the ship's surgeon. But who would protect Nelie from the surgeon?

When Stuart faltered, Belle said, "I can make a contribution to this effort, Captain Stuart."

"More likely you'll be underfoot."

"Sir, I will not be underfoot. You have my word on that."

"And you won't roam the deck, questioning the crew as to their responsibilities or previous adventures."

"Not if you forbid it."

"I do. This cabin shall be your home, and you'll need my permission to leave it."

Belle nodded. "I agree to your terms."

"And no fencing."

"Sir?"

"You heard what I said. No fencing, though there's a barrel of foils on the quarterdeck. Those weapons are for learning how to kill people, not score points."

"Even if I'm requested to participate?"

"Especially if you are asked to participate. I will speak to those who believe a rapier is a proper weapon. I know who they are, and I will remind them of what fools they are."

Belle bristled.

"Mr. Belle, do you actually think there will be room to maneuver and engage in sophisticated blade work on any ship during the heat of battle?"

"Well, perhaps not." Belle brightened. "Of course, it's always best to remain sharp for the next encounter. I, myself, practice everyday."

Stuart turned to the table dominating the cabin and

opened a drawer. "You Belles are big on documents." Stuart produced a sheet of paper, quill, and ink bottle. "You shall write that you are doing this by your own hand, and you will include all the restrictions I laid on you, or you shall not sail with us."

Belle reached for the paper, but Stuart pulled it away. "You need a witness." Hearing the hammering and sawing on the other side of the cabin door, Stuart added, "And it won't be one of my men."

"Very well."

Belle left the ship to the sound of the bosun shouting instructions to those in the hold. Before the *Mary Stewart* sailed, there would be near one hundred members of the crew onboard, along with one hundred kegs of whiskey and rum sequestered in the hold.

Following Belle to the gangway, Stuart called after him. "And the witness must be a notary."

Denis turned around and walked backwards in the direction of East Bay. "And you're not to leave without me."

"Oh," said Stuart, rather cheerily, "we'll do our best to try."

While Belle was ashore, Stuart met with the other two captains of his line. The three men spoke in Stuart's cabin and surveyed charts of Ocracoke Island, part of the Outer Banks. One of the captains, Churchill, had been stopped in the past by Blackbeard, so he was ready and willing to follow Stuart into battle. The other captain, Ward, didn't think it was any of his business.

"Pirates are everyone's business," said Churchill.

"We've all been pirates at one time or another." Ward rolled up his sleeves to reveal his tattoos.

"Look, Jake," said Stuart, "all I'm asking you to do is to follow me to North Carolina. Blackbeard is sailing with more than one ship, and so shall I. You won't even have to discharge your current cargo."

Ward shook his head. "Unless I'm attacked, Captain, I no longer engage in combat. I've had a gutful of that."

"You know," said Churchill, "you've been riding too easy out there on blue water under the flag of Stuart & Company."

"I don't go looking for trouble," said Ward, addressing his comments to Churchill. "When we approach any port, we are under full sail and approach just before nightfall."

The other captain sneered at him. "I've never believed those tales of your ship's ability to round-to."

Stuart turned to Churchill. "You have your orders. We sail with the tide. See how soon you can make ready."

"Aye, aye, Captain." As Churchill went out the cabin door, he shot another look at Ward. "You can count on me."

Once Churchill had left, Stuart explained his predicament. "You know this is my fiancée Blackbeard has taken."

"This is true?" Ward appeared surprised.

Stuart nodded.

"I never thought of you as the marrying kind, Captain."

"Neither did I until I met Nelie Belle."

Ward nodded. "I understand those feelings. I have suffered them myself."

"And you know that I'm not in the habit of begging."

"And you shall not have to. I will have my ship rigged within the hour and we shall follow you to the Outer Banks."

Denis Belle returned with the notary, the paperwork was signed, and a copy placed in a safe in the warehouse on Stuart's Bridge. Moments later, Samuel Chase entered the cabin to announce they were ready to sail and that the harbormaster was ready to lead them out of the harbor.

Denis Belle turned to Stuart. "I thought you knew this harbor's every nook and cranny."

"That I do, sir, but I'm not the sort to pick another man's pocket. The harbormaster has a job to do."

Chase grinned. "Not to mention the harbormaster loves to lead any ship James Stuart is piloting out of the harbor. Sometimes he even takes the long way round." Chase looked at Stuart. "And the flag, sir?"

"Hoist the red one and do so before we leave anchorage."

Denis shuddered. "Really? No quarter?"

Belle took a seat on his sea chest. The red flag, or what had become known as the Jolly Roger, was a corruption of "pretty red" in French, and commonly flew with a black background and a variety of white skulls and crossbones. But Stuart had ordered raising the red flag, a completely different matter.

"Mr. Belle, people need to understand that I'm serious

about locating your sister-in-law, and if you don't believe Blackbeard has spies in Charles Town, then, sir, you are a fool."

"But—but I've heard the no-quarter flag only makes those on the other ship fight even harder, since there will be no quarter given to any survivors."

Stuart came out from behind the table. "Mr. Belle, I'm not in the habit of having my orders questioned, and certainly not by any landsman."

"No, no," said Denis, looking up from where he sat on his chest. "I was not questioning your orders. I was trying to understand."

"No, you weren't, and the next time you misunderstand one of my orders, perhaps you should wait until we are alone to question my tactics."

"Cast off lines," called out Chase.

From the wharf where the *Mary Stewart* was moored, the lines slipped away and the harbormaster guided the ship into the harbor. Kyrle stood at the helm, tending the wheel; beside him stood the African, Alexander. From the hold came the sound of additional railings being fitted into place to restrain the kegs of rum and whiskey, and watching from the hatch, an abstainer with a pistol. One of those maneuvering lengths of lumber below and in very tight quarters was Rodney Wickham, who had toured the deck earlier in the day and familiarized himself with the swivel guns mounted on the bow and the quarterdeck.

Samuel Chase glanced at Stuart's cabin. "That man is to become your brother-in-law?"

"Yes, and once I'm married, I'm expected to attend

the Huguenot church—the French have a morning and afternoon service, if you didn't know—and dine Sundays at the Belles'."

The quartermaster nodded. "My mother-in-law insists I do the same whenever ashore. Is this the Belle house on Meeting?"

"That's the one."

"That's quite a house, Captain."

"Yes, but it's the mistress of that house who's to be reckoned with."

The quartermaster watched Charles Town fall away aft: all the buildings along East Bay, the harbor with its ships at anchorage, and the white-tipped peninsula still covered with oyster shells; all disappearing in the orange-yellow light of the setting sun.

Chase had seen plenty of ports in his day, and he could recognize a harbor with an unlimited future, but all that was on his mind was the anticipation of blue water outside the Charles Town Bar.

"You know, Captain, sometimes I think a sailor gives up too much when he weds and goes ashore to live."

"Mr. Chase, I don't think you'll find a single sailor who disagrees with you on that point."

ELEVEN

Once they were underway, Alexander dragged a pirate by the name of Robert Winder into Stuart's cabin. Though the man appeared lame, Alexander showed him no mercy, throwing the pirate to the deck in front of the table where the captain sat. Alexander closed the door and posted himself there, shutting out most of the noise from the quarterdeck and the hold. On the deck, Winder rolled around, moaning and gripping his knee.

"He wasn't all that hard to find, Captain," said the cannon master. "In every bar along the waterfront, he kept whining about how Blackbeard had abandoned him." Alexander laughed at the man withering in pain on the deck in front of the table. "Sail with Edward Teach, what do you expect—cakes and tea?"

"Who is this?" asked Belle, rising from where he sat on his sea chest.

Stuart asked the man on the deck if he had been a member of Blackbeard's crew when Charles Town had been held hostage. Winder only moaned, rolled around, and gripped his knee with both hands. Belle glanced at Stuart, then, leaving his seat on the chest, helped the injured man into a chair across from Stuart.

"Much obliged, sir," said the injured man.

Stuart spoke in French to Belle as the Frenchman returned to his chest. "You know that I'll have to clap you in irons when we go ashore."

Belle was taken aback. "And why is that?" Denis spoke the same language.

"Because you're too much the gentleman, and it tends to make you irrational." Stuart turned his attention to the injured pirate across the table from him. "So who shot you?" he asked in English.

"Teach."

"Well," said Alexander from the door, "it would appear Blackbeard needs to work on his aim."

Winder winced when he turned in the chair to look at the large, black man standing behind him. "The way you see me is how Teach left me, so I left him."

"Deserted his command, did you?" Stuart leaned back in his chair and clumped his boots on the table.

"That I did. Your captain shoots you without cause, well, I'm quits with Teach."

"Surely, you must've given offense," suggested Denis Belle.

"Sir, I did nothing of the sort," said Winder. "We were sitting in the captain's cabin talking about the blockade, and Teach pulls out one of his pistols, holds it under the table, and shoots me." To Stuart, he said, "You know that leather belt Teach wears across his chest?"

Stuart nodded. There were usually three pistols

in Blackbeard's bandolier, not to mention Teach was several inches taller than most men, truly an imposing figure with his long, black hair and flowing beard.

"Well," went on Winder, "I was just sitting there and Teach shoots me. From where I lay on the deck, trying to stanch the flow of blood, I asked the captain why he'd done that."

"And his explanation?" asked Belle, scooting to the edge of his sea chest.

Stuart sighed and looked at Alexander. The African shook his head and rolled his eyes. In the relative silence, sounds from the quarterdeck and the hold, though muffled, could be heard: Samuel Chase shouting something about maintaining mast-to-mast distance and wood being hammered into place in the hold.

Winder gave his attention to the man who provided the best audience. "The captain said he needed to shoot someone every once in a while just to maintain good order."

"My God," said Belle. "How barbaric."

But Stuart would not let the injured pirate get wound up. "So why did Teach come to Charles Town?"

Winder shrugged. "The usual, stopping ships, and there are plenty of ships to stop outside the Charles Town Bar."

"But Teach wanted something he couldn't find on those ships, didn't he?"

Winder said nothing.

Stuart pulled his boots off the table and clumped them to the deck. "Let's see if we can reason this out. Blackbeard spends the winter on the Main, but before he leaves, he gives his crew one last liberty because there's no bordellos like the ones on New Providence."

Winder nodded as if hearing this for the first time. "Yes, sir. That's what he did."

"And on New Providence everyone drinks themselves into a stupor, but before they do, they fall in bed with whores, and these whores have syphilis. Two weeks later everyone has the itch. That's when Teach's fleet arrives off the Bar."

Absentmindedly, Winder scratched his crotch. "I guess you could say that."

"And if you need medicine, every seaman worth his salt knows the most poorly defended harbor is the one at Charles Town. Its guns are effective only if a ship enters the harbor, so Teach could demand anything he wanted, as long as he remained outside the Bar."

"But we harmed no one, and once the captain received the medicine, the passengers were returned safe and sound."

"In their drawers," said Alexander from the door.

Winder chuckled. "Yes, that was a sight to see, especially the ladies."

"No harm done?" asked Denis Belle, rising off his chest.

"Sit down, Mr. Belle," ordered Stuart.

Belle did so.

Now Winder tried to curry favor with the Scot. "Beg pardon, sir, but we were under orders to allow your ships to pass. Blackbeard respects your flag, Captain Stuart."

"Did you see the color of the flag on our mast?"

Winder nodded. "'Tis red for sure."

"And now we need to know what plans Teach has for the immediate future."

Winder looked around the room and lowered his voice. "He's headed to Bath Town to ask for a pardon from Governor Eden."

"Not Virginia?"

"Oh, no. Governor Spotswood would hang Teach, and probably without benefit of a trial."

"Why North Carolina?" asked Belle.

Winder shrugged. "Everyone knows there's no way the governor can patrol the Outer Banks, so Eden looks the other way and allows us to trade with his people."

Stuart asked, "Have you heard anything about a young girl being kidnapped from one of the Cooper River plantations?"

Winder shook his head and shook it too quickly. "No, no, nothing like that."

"She would've been under Philip Morton's protection."

"Oh, no, sir. Nothing about any ladies on the *Queen Anne's Revenge.*"

Stuart spoke to the African at the door. "Alexander, why don't you hold Mr. Winder up by his bad leg and see if you can shake anything out of him."

Denis gasped, and when Alexander stepped over to the chair, Winder scrambled to his feet and clumped around to the far side of the table to stand near Stuart. Alexander came after him.

Looking at the Scot who remained in his chair, the pirate said, "I've told you everything I know, Captain, truly I have. There's no more to tell."

Stuart raised his hand, stopping Alexander who had followed Winder around the table. Gesturing at Belle, he said, "I forgot. We have a gentleman present."

That made Winder direct his pleas to Belle, talking across Stuart. "I pray that you'll have mercy on me, sir, an injured man, and one who wishes to have a pardon granted by the governor."

Belle didn't know what to say, looking from Winder to Stuart and back again.

Stuart asked Alexander to summon the quartermaster, and moments later, Samuel Chase entered the cabin, followed by the cabin boy. Before the door closed, there could be heard shouts between one crew member to another; someone laughed, another hooted, all sounds of men thrilled to be at sea again.

"Ship's position and status?" asked Stuart.

"Just cleared the Bar. Heading's north by northeast. Churchill's on our starboard, Ward's on our port. No ships sighted as of yet, Captain. We're maintaining twelve miles mast to masthead, and the red flag has been lowered until we sight one of Teach's ships. Ward and Churchill know to approach every ship for news of Blackbeard. Status of *Mary Stewart:* still working out the cobwebs, as a fighting ship, that is."

From the corner of the table, Alexander said, "Once we're finished with Winder, I'll make sure every cannon crew acquits themselves like veterans."

"By the way, Captain," asked Chase, "the men want to know how much for each pirate killed."

"Tell Kyrle to set a course for Bath Town." Stuart looked at the lame pirate who stood on his side of the table.

Winder nodded.

Stuart returned his attention to the quartermaster. "As for killing pirates, I'll post something. Tell them to check the door in about an hour." He gestured at Denis Belle. "Mr. Chase, would you take Mr. Belle to the bow so he can observe the progress of our ship? Take your cane along, Mr. Belle, so you can enjoy your stroll." Leaning against the bulkhead behind him was the Frenchman's cane.

Denis stood. "I don't need to be dismissed, Captain Stuart."

"I disagree," said Stuart. In rapid-fire French, he added, "You can't control your mouth, and because of that, you put your sister-in-law in danger."

Denis glanced at Winder. "Then I will keep my mouth shut. On my word of honor."

"One word," said Stuart, holding up his index finger.

Belle nodded and returned to his chest.

In English, Stuart said to the African, "We need answers."

Alexander grabbed the injured pirate and flipped him upside down. Winder screamed. He was being held upside down by his injured leg.

Stuart turned to Belle. "Just nod if you acknowledge that this is necessary to locate the girl."

Face pale, even for a Belle, Denis nodded.

When Winder passed out, Alexander dropped him to the deck on the other side of the table. Samuel Chase had the cabin boy fetch a bucket of water, and it wasn't long before Winder was revived.

Peering over the table at the man lying in the puddle

of water, Stuart asked, "I want to know the disposition of the young woman kidnapped from the Cooper River plantation."

Winder said he didn't know anything about her.

"Alexander?"

The African reached for Winder again.

The lame man scooted across the deck, sliding through the puddle of water. "No, no, please. The lady wished to be kidnapped."

"Women on Teach's ships? I know better than that. He only takes them there to bed them."

"Oh, yes," said Winder, nodding vigorously. "But this girl fancied herself the next Anne Bonny."

Stuart studied the man on the deck. "And I think you're holding out on me."

Winder smiled. "Well, Captain, it would appear you have an interest in what I know."

Alexander stepped over and kicked him in the knee. Winder screamed, Belle gasped, but the others in the cabin simply waited for Winder to calm down. Chase threw another bucket of water so Winder never had the chance to pass out. Still, it took a few minutes before the pirate could speak.

"You . . . you guarantee my safety if . . . if I speak against my former captain and my mates."

Stuart nodded. "You have my word."

"You have no plans to kill me, maim me, or maroon me?"

"Nothing." Stuart gestured at Belle. "On this you have the word of a gentleman. Just tell us where the girl is."

Winder smiled from the deck. "I imagine I would speak better if I was in the chair."

Stuart nodded to Alexander, who picked up Winder and thumped him down in a chair opposite Stuart.

When the injured man stopped grimacing, he had another request: "Might do with a shot of whiskey for the pain, if you please, Captain."

Stuart got to his feet, took a bottle from a locked cabinet in the corner of the cabin, and poured the whiskey. He handed the glass to Winder. "You have one minute, and then Alexander is going to tie you to a rope, throw you overboard, and drag you from the stern. You know there are sharks in these waters."

"No need for that." Winder gulped down the whiskey. "My allegiance is to you and your ship now."

"Well?"

Placing the empty glass on the table, Winder asked, "You've heard of Major Stede Bonnet of the Barbados militia?"

Stuart glanced· at Chase.

"Captain of the *Revenge*," said the quartermaster. "During the blockade, Bonnet was a guest of Blackbeard on the *Queen Anne's Revenge*."

"Guest?" asked Stuart, plainly puzzled.

"Bonnet doesn't seem to know much about pirating."

"You're saying Teach seized Bonnet's ship."

"No, sir. Made him a shipmate. Someone from the *Queen Anne's Revenge* now sails Bonnet's ship."

Winder joined in. "Major Bonnet is to meet with Governor Eden and apply for a pardon for Teach and his entire crew. Once the pardon's granted, Teach will ask the governor to marry him and the girl from the Cooper River plantation."

"Whether the girl wishes to marry him or not," asked Stuart.

Winder leaned back in his chair, quite satisfied with himself. "Well, I don't remember any woman ever turning down Blackbeard."

TWELVE

Whenever the stern lantern was extinguished, every sailor who had sailed with James Stuart knew better than to bother the captain as he stood in the stern, looking out to sea. This was where Stuart could think; certainly not in his cabin. That was too much like being on land. Besides, there was little for him to do. When the *Mary Stewart* was not in action, the quartermaster ran the ship; the Irishman, Kyrle, stood at the helm.

As Stuart stood in the darkness, listening to the *Mary Stewart* slash her way through the water—they had a good wind behind them—eight bells rung, signaling the beginning of a new day, and there was the constant sound of Alexander running the cannon crews through their paces. There were two arrays, one on the main deck, the other on the lower deck, and what made the African so valuable was that he could have either array fire, reload and fire again, all in less than one minute, putting tremendous pressure on any opponent.

That was the difference between Stuart and Blackbeard: the Scot had more cannon, Teach had more men. Stuart wanted to hang back, blasting away in an attempt to demast an opponent; Blackbeard wished to frighten you to death, and if you didn't tremble in your boots when you saw several hundred pirates screaming and waving their cutlasses, and led by an oversized man with his beard on fire, well, you were as crazy as Blackbeard.

So, with the wind whipping through the fabric of his shirt, James Stuart stood alone in the stern and stared up at the stars, the first fixed points he had learned for crossing blue water. Those same stars had led him to Charles Town and his first sighting of Nelie Belle, and after finding work in the harbor, Stuart noticed, every day, that his angel stood on the wall overlooking the harbor.

Screwing up his courage, Stuart approached her and began identifying the various ships in the harbor. Nelie pretended to care. Nelie did not care. She remained heartbroken over the loss of her family, and spent some time every day, checking the ships at anchorage and hoping her parents, brother, and the baby would somehow find their way to the Huguenot sanctuary in Charles Town.

Evenings on the stern also reminded Stuart of his adventures on the Main where his crews took anything they wanted, well, at least from the Spanish and the French. Truly, the life of a pirate tugged at a man's heart like no other. There were no women, no children, and no responsibilities; everyone voted on their next victim, even voted whether Stuart would continue as captain. It was a pure democracy in which the inmates ran the asylum.

It would be difficult to leave blue water, but not if you remembered the shipmates who had been ripped to pieces by cannon fire, taken away by disease, or, more likely, killed in a barroom brawl. Because of this, the life of a landlubber began to make more sense, and Stuart never forgot what the old black man with the milky eye had told him: that Sir Henry Morgan had invested in sugar plantations instead of spending his share of the booty in brothels. So, it was on the Spanish Main that Stuart found himself saving his share and thinking of Nelie Belle; not that her family would ever agree to such a union, but a man could always dream.

For that reason, whenever Stuart found a ship headed for Charles Town, he would have a letter wrapped in oilskin and ready for delivery to Nelie Belle of Belle Mercantile. There was an eight for the man who made the delivery, and the expense of the eight was to be posted to Stuart's account, an account established with Belle Mercantile long before he ever left Carolina.

Though it was presumptuous on his part to write to an unmarried woman without her family's permission, Stuart was nevertheless proud of how well he wrote, all attributed to his childhood in Glasgow. For that reason, one of his letters included a vivid description of rounding Cape Horn and having to wear every stitch of clothing he owned so he wouldn't freeze to death. Another letter described the huge turtles of the Galapagos Islands.

They were lies. All lies. Stuart had heard such tales from sailors in the taverns of New Providence—because the only way he could make his fortune was by going to sea and serving under a captain who had a license to plunder ships flying foreign flags. Both Blackbeard and Stuart served under Benjamin Hornigold, and Hornigold had single-handedly talked hundreds of pirates into accepting the king's pardon and giving up piracy. One of those accepting the pardon was James Stuart. One who did not was Blackbeard. And when Stuart, Chase, Kyrle, and Alexander returned to Charles Town, Stuart was quick to notice that Nelie Belle wore no wedding band. The Scot practically danced down the street. He had a chance! He really had a chance.

One day, Stuart finally had the courage to ask, "Tell me, Miss Belle, if I might be so bold to ask, but why is it that a handsome young woman like you is not married? You must be pursued by numerous suitors, especially those who simply walk in off East Bay." Stuart figured the girl for about sixteen years of age, and though he was much older, it was time to make his move.

Nelie Belle's face was porcelain white, her eyes blue, her hair raven black, and she had a marvelous smile. Under her plain, dark dress, Nelie wore an ankle-length chemise, and to protect her dress, she wore an apron complete with bib, but she did not wear stays because of the need to stretch and bend to retrieve merchandise for her customers.

The dress did not have pockets but slits through which Nelie could access her pockets, a separate article of clothing tied around her waist, over the chemise and under the dress. In those pockets were coins, straight pins stuck in a cushion, and scissors. Pinned to the bib of her apron was the Huguenot cross: a Maltese cross with a dove attached at the bottom.

"That, Captain Stuart, *is* a rather bold question for a young man to ask a young woman."

"I see. Are you saying it is a rather bold question for a privateer to ask a woman of high-born birth?"

"Sir," said Nelie, with no hint of humor, "it is you who are fitting people into categories. It's obvious that I am a young woman and you are a young man. Beyond that, what is there to know?"

"Oh," said Stuart with a laugh, "but it cannot be that easy. You must defer to those in your family to make these distinctions clear to you."

"As I will do when I have children of my own."

"And if your daughter brings home a privateer?"

"Oh, that's easy. I would simply tell him to return to sea."

"But, Miss, what of the privateer who becomes a landsman?"

"Then, sir, by definition he would no longer be a privateer."

Once, when Nelie was assisting Stuart with a purchase, her sister walked through the store and right past the sea captain.

Because of this, Stuart asked, "Why is it that your sister is not as charming as you, Miss Belle?"

Nelie glanced toward the rear of the store where her sister had disappeared. Catherine always wore stays, even to bed at night, and nothing about Catherine was plain. Her dress was often short, open in the front below the waist and ending at the knees, the top garment over several petticoats reaching her shoes.

"My sister is burdened with the responsibilities of our family, Captain Stuart, but she knows I will treat you fairly and honestly while you are in our store. Her smile is not required."

The Scot scanned the room in which every shelf or table was stacked high with goods. Belle Mercantile was busy, people making purchases, coming and going. It was noisy and distracting, that is, unless he was speaking to Nelie Belle.

"You certainly don't appear to lack for trade."

"Yes," said the girl, smiling again. "It's a wondrous thing to work for an uncle who understands the proper pricing and selection of goods."

Stuart surveyed the store again. "But I hardly ever see your uncle in the store."

"Ah, well, that is because his office is in the rear, like the helm, where the store is run."

"Helm?" Stuart smiled. "And what do you know of ships and their operation, Miss Belle?"

"Captain Stuart, are you telling me that you've forgotten all those hours we spent as children across the street? It was there that you pointed out the difference between frigates, sloops, and corvettes. I received a considerable education standing on the harbor wall, an education that helped me adapt to clerking where many of the customers are seafaring men. Why, I have even been allowed to tend the tiller when we sail upriver to Cooper Hill."

"You know, Miss Belle," said Stuart, leaning into the counter and lowering his voice, "Stuart & Company owns boats similar to the one on which you have operated the tiller."

"Why, of course," said Nelie, stepping back and tucking her hands behind her. "I see you racing around the harbor in them. It reminds me of that day you took me sailing."

"Yes," said Stuart, glancing toward the rear of the building, "I believe it was your sister who forbade you to ever sail with me again."

"Well," said Nelie with another of her infectious smiles, "you have to admit I did a great deal of screaming as you maneuvered in and out of all those huge ships. They certainly don't look that large from the harbor wall. Still, it was not your fault that word of my hysteria reached the ear of my sister. And, of course, these days everything must be done properly."

Stuart didn't know what she meant and it must've showed on his face.

Amused, Nelie asked, "Why, Captain Stuart, you really don't understand social conventions? Well, that will certainly hamper your marrying the woman of your choice."

And Stuart realized, from his time spent among some very clever women in a variety of seaports, that signals were being sent by this raven-haired beauty. He just had to interpret the message. Still, like any man, Stuart did not appreciate subtleties, and his conversation remained rather straightforward and to the point.

"Tell me, Miss Belle, what is it that a young woman like yourself looks for in a man? A suitable one, that is."

A sly look crossed the girl's face. "Oh, I think he would have to be rather handsome and be a very good dancer."

"Miss Belle, now you are toying with me."

Nelie laughed. "And, you, sir, would be correct. What a woman looks for in a man is a certain handsomeness, but he must be able to provide for his family, which would include owning a proper home where children can be raised. And be God-fearing."

Stuart's mind appeared to be elsewhere.

"Captain Stuart?"

"Oh, begging your pardon, Miss Belle, but you set my mind off on a tangent."

"I'm sorry to interrupt your thoughts, Captain Stuart, but anyone I would marry would have to attend church regularly. Otherwise, how would my husband be able to guide our children on the road to righteousness?"

"You mean the Huguenot Church?"

"Captain Stuart, you take things too literally. There is much flexibility in social intercourse, and that also applies to the church. For example, if a couple such as you and I were to wed"—the girl blushed and glanced at the floor—"we could attend either church. Your John Knox studied under our John Calvin, so we are both Calvinists." And very quickly, Nelie added a dose of dry history: "You may not know, but Presbyterians, Congregationalists, and Huguenots built the second church in Charles Town, called the Presbyterian Church or the White Meeting, which is how Meeting Street received its name. The Huguenot Church was built ten years later. I assume you attend the Circular Church?"

"Well, it is the law," said Stuart, smiling.

"Oh, a privateer who respects our laws? Now that must be an interesting man to get to know."

"Miss Belle, are you toying with me again?"

"To some degree," said Nelie, grinning, "but you are a handsome man, Captain Stuart, and occasionally I wish to see you smile."

And Stuart became determined that the girl would see much more of him, so, the following day, he purchased a lot on Meeting Street where the wall had so recently come down. A week later, carpenters began building the first single house, a building Stuart thought would adapt well from Barbados to Charles Town.

Still, it would appear that the former privateer had much to learn. Stuart might own the correct clothing, cut his hair properly, shave, and clean under his fingernails, but the day after being involved in a fistfight, Stuart appeared at Belle Mercantile sporting a shiner and a split lip. Nelie was concerned; Stuart was not. It had been a rather good fight.

"Captain Stuart, are you sure you're all right?"

He grinned. "You should've seen the other fellow."

"I don't understand. You act as if you enjoyed fighting. Perchance you were drinking again?"

"That's how most fights begin." Stuart leaned over the counter and whispered, "Frenchies do fight, Miss Belle. One of the Huguenots gave as good as he got."

The girl backed away, hand to mouth. She was speechless.

The head clerk, Jacob Huger, wandered over. "Is there something I might help you find, Captain Stuart?"

The Scot came off the counter, and when he looked again at the girl, he realized he'd frightened her. "I'm sorry if what I said distressed you, Miss Belle, but it was over the honor of a lady that we fought."

"Sir," said Nelie, sweeping down the aisle behind the counter, "there are no ladies at the Carolina Tavern. Of that, I am certain." And she disappeared into the rear of the store.

"Sir?" asked Huger again. The thin man wore a severe black suit and a white shirt with a rather tight collar.

Stuart finally focused on him. "What?"

"Do you have a list of goods you wish to have sent over to your warehouse or will you be shopping from memory?"

Stuart pulled just such a list from his pocket. "All this can be sent to the *Mary Stewart.*"

"Yes, sir." Huger gave a slight bow. "Within the hour."

But Stuart was staring at the door in the rear of the shop. "I must've given the young lady offense."

"Well, sir," said the clerk, lowering his voice, "I cannot tell you the number of times Mrs. Catherine Belle has told me that her sister has a weak constitution."

"A weak constitution?" Stuart returned his attention to Huger. "But look at the number of sickly seasons she's survived."

"I'm in total agreement with you, sir. I'm only repeating what the Belles have told me about Miss Nelie's constitution."

Glancing at the rear door again, Stuart asked if the clerk had a piece of paper and a writing instrument. While Huger gathered the material, Stuart gathered his thoughts, and when Huger returned, Stuart composed a note and asked for an envelope, all to be put on his account.

"Sir," said the clerk, "this is a request I am happy to oblige."

"Very well," said Stuart, folding the note several times. Not having a way to seal the envelope, Stuart folded the note in a way he could fold the envelope repeatedly over the sheet of paper. He handed the envelope to the clerk. "Please see that Miss Belle receives this."

"Yes, sir."

Huger stood there, and Stuart stood there, and finally the sea captain asked, "Would you mind delivering the note while I know Miss Belle is still in the store."

"Why, yes, sir," said Huger, and he disappeared into the rear of the shop.

Stuart stood there for a moment, then turned on his heel and stepped out on East Bay. Before returning to his ship, he went down the street to the Carolina Tavern.

The tavern owner was not pleased to see him. "Will there be fighting again, sir?" asked the owner, usually a jolly fellow.

Stuart counted out some pieces of eight on the tavern's bar. "This is to pay for any damages from last night's fight."

"Oh, thank you, sir. Thank you very much." Once the owner had counted the eights, he became his jolly self again. "How about a drink, sir, on the house?" Filling a glass, he placed it on the bar in front of the Scot.

"No, thank you," said Stuart, as if looking through the tavern wall and seeing into a business farther down East Bay. "Enjoy the drink yourself—from the money I gave you."

"Very well, sir."

The smiling man downed the drink as Stuart left, which turned out to be a most inopportune moment. As Stuart held open the door, the tavern owner's wife came through, and her eyes fell upon her husband drinking from his own stock. The tavern owner lost his jolliness and didn't regain it until several days later.

THIRTEEN

Less than a half hour after James Stuart had spoken to Nelie in Belle Mercantile, Samuel Chase entered the Scot's cabin on the *Mary Stewart*. Stuart was engaged in some figuring at the table, using a piece of graphite wrapped in string that he could peel back as the graphite point wore down. A piece of India rubber lay nearby to remove the graphite marks made in error.

"I think it's time we move our operation ashore. That way, we can promote Churchill to captain and build an office on the bridge."

"There's more good news," said the quartermaster. "Denis Belle has come aboard. Perhaps those snooty French want to do business with Stuart & Company. That would make building an office on the bridge much more feasible."

"Then show him in."

When Denis Belle was ushered into the cabin, Stuart had cleared the table of his figuring and was looking through his wine selection. It was not a large selection, and in truth, Stuart was a whiskey man. Never one to pass up an opportunity for a drink, Samuel Chase took up a position at the cabin door.

"Please have a seat, Mr. Belle," said Stuart, without turning around. "I was looking for the correct wine."

"I would rather stand, sir, if you don't mind."

Stuart returned the bottle to the wooden locker and faced the Frenchman. "Then, I take it this is a formal meeting."

"Yes." Belle gestured with his cane at Samuel Chase. "Formal and private."

"I have no secrets from Samuel."

Denis gave him a tight little smile. "Well, I just might."

"Then be gone, Samuel, and close the door behind you."

"I'll be right outside, Captain."

Once the door closed, Belle said, "Not a very trusting fellow, is he?"

Stuart shrugged. "Well, he is English and you are French."

"But you're a Scot."

"That's true, but with the signing of the Treaty of Unification, Samuel and I have agreed to let bygones be bygones."

Belle stepped to the table and laid down the note Stuart had written only minutes before. There was no longer any envelope, but the sheet of paper had been repeatedly folded. "Did you write this, sir?"

"I did."

"And you intended it for my sister-in-law?"

"That is also correct."

"Perhaps you should have transacted such business through me."

"Mr. Belle, I'm sorry if I've offended your family, but when I saw how I had upset your sister-in-law, I wanted to make my apology immediately."

"I understand." Belle gestured at the note with his cane. "Besides the apology, which is accepted, there is the matter of the other information in the note." Denis picked up the note and read: "The lady in question was your sister."

"Yes?"

"What were you referring to, sir, when you spoke of my wife so familiarly?"

"Sir, the correspondence was between your sister-in-law and me."

"Sir, you referred to my wife in your note and I will have your answer or satisfaction."

Stuart studied the man. "Let me tell you how this is to play out, Mr. Belle. You can ask for satisfaction, and that is within your right, but I will have the choice of weapons." He jerked a thumb at the wall where two broadswords hung, cross swords. "Those are the weapons we shall use and we will take them out on deck and use them immediately. There will be no seconds, no doctors, and no time to gather a select number of your circle to watch my humiliation. But it will be a quick end to this dispute so that one of us may return to our business."

Belle stared at the broadswords on the wall. They were straight-bladed, double-edged, and with a basket-hilt to protect the hand. The blade was almost three feet long and the total weight appeared to be close to ten pounds. "No gentleman would ever use such a weapon."

"Sir, I am no gentleman." Stuart gestured at the cane in Belle's hand. "You can thrash me if you care to try, but if you're unsuccessful, or you should fail to agree to my terms, then I am prepared to call you a coward in every gathering place along this waterfront."

Belle bristled. "Then it's best your quartermaster heard none of this."

"Oh, but I did," said Chase, from the other side of the cabin door. "I heard everything, and though my captain is a lousy Scot, he is very good with a broadsword, and your wife will be a widow before nightfall."

"Sir," said Belle, speaking to the voice on the other side of the door, "are you threatening me?"

"Oh, no, sir, Mr. Belle. I have no idea who slit your throat and threw your body overboard, but this is a rough harbor for a gentleman to navigate."

Belle spoke to Stuart. "Then, I shall await you on shore and we shall handle this as gentlemen."

Chase's voice came again. "All I hear is a dead man talking."

Denis held back his coat on both sides. "You see, sir, I am not armed."

"Well," said Stuart, "that is rather stupid. When you board what you consider a pirate ship, you should come armed. There are many who would lift your purse without a thought. Is that why the Belle family does little or no business with Stuart & Company—the fact that our company is not run by gentlemen? I have it on good authority that your family does business with others who are not highborn, such as the Welshman who runs your factory on the Neck."

"No," said Belle, "my wife says . . ." He stopped. "Your prices are too high, and that is why we do little business with you."

"Oh, you don't care to pay the pirate insurance." Stuart walked around the table to where Belle stood. "Still, you must be aware of the fact that none of my ships have been boarded in the last few years."

"There are those who say you are in league with pirates."

"Even a better reason to do business with Stuart & Company."

"Sir, I came aboard as any other husband would do when he believed his wife slandered."

"Sir, your wife is French and living in an English port. She should be used to being maligned. I, myself, ignore those who chide me for not wearing a kilt." Stuart evaluated Belle. "That is, unless they become a nuisance. Now, how have I become a nuisance to you, Mr. Belle? I know your reputation with both sword and pistol, and I must say it's excellent."

Belle pointed at the note.

"Samuel," said Stuart, raising his voice, "a little privacy, if you don't mind."

"Aye, aye, Captain."

Stuart and Belle waited until the sound of the quartermaster's boots faded away, then Stuart asked, "What I want to know is whether Nelie will be clerking in Belle Mercantile as she has done in the past?"

Denis didn't know where that came from but stated that it wasn't any of Stuart's business.

"I believe it is," said the Scot, "and if you cannot guarantee that Nelie will continue to work in the store as she has done previously, then it's time to select our weapons." Stuart returned to the other side of the table and reached for one of the broadswords.

"Sir, you are becoming much too familiar with my sister-in-law."

"I knew her as a child, Mr. Belle. Every day that she crossed East Bay, I made myself available to identify the different ships in the harbor. I count her as a childhood friend."

"Which only reinforces the concern of my family."

Stuart took down the first of the broadswords, turned around, and laid the weapon on the table. "Well, in a few minutes that won't matter, will it? One of us will be dead."

Belle watched him take down the other sword. "Captain Stuart, you cannot address a young woman by her first name. It is much too familiar."

Stuart laid the second broadsword on the table, picked up a rag, and began to wipe the first one clean. He hoped Belle could not tell that both weapons had not been used in a very long time.

As he cleaned the blade, he said, "Nelie gave me permission to call her by her first name. Prior to that, I always referred to her as 'Miss Belle,' but she insists on calling me 'Captain Stuart,' and for that reason, I now call her 'Miss Belle' once again."

Denis watched the former pirate wipe the weapon clean, then use the rag on the second broadsword. He said, "Nelie cannot give such permission. She is not of age."

Stuart gestured at the broadsword on the table. "Please, Mr. Belle, it is my choice of weapons, but it is your choice of the two."

Belle picked up the weapon, turning it one way, then the other, feeling the weight in his hand. What manner of man would use such a weapon?

"So," said Stuart, placing the second broadsword on the table for Belle to examine, "we are to fight a duel because you refuse to guarantee that your sister-in-law will be allowed to return to her work at Belle Mercantile. I think you are about to have more trouble than you bargained for when you first came aboard, and you shall not be able to hold me accountable."

Belle put down the broadsword but did not pick up the other one. "Nelie is my uncle's ward," he said rather lamely.

"Still, that's the reason for the duel—because I'm about to tell you what the note meant, and you will have no other cause to fret, except for me telling you whom to employ in your store."

Belle appeared eager to hear. "You will, sir?"

"I shall. Last night, a man came in the Carolina Tavern, and when he had more than a few drinks, this man, an Indian trader, spoke disparagingly of your family, in particular your wife."

"If you only give me his name."

Stuart chuckled and told Belle the man's name.

The Frenchman nodded. "Then I shall seek redress elsewhere." He turned to go.

"But what about our duel?" Stuart gestured at the broadswords lying on the table.

"Sir, I understand you were defending the honor of

my wife, and I appreciate what you have done. I will take my complaint elsewhere." Belle turned to the door again.

"But the man is no longer in Charles Town."

Denis opened the cabin door. "I care not whether he has returned to the frontier or when he returns, but if he ever reenters Charles Town, I will thrash him within an inch of his life."

"But you'll never see him again."

"And why is that?"

"He was pressed into service on one of His Majesty's ships, and they set sail this morning to circumnavigate the globe. This man is no seaman, and I doubt he will make it as far as Cape Horn."

Belle did not know what to say.

"So," said Stuart, gesturing at the swords, "we return to the issue before us."

Denis was unsure as to the nature of their quarrel. It would appear Stuart had curried favor with the Belle family by defending the honor of his wife. Or he had despoiled Nelie by his constant attentions. It was hard to say.

"Does Nelie know you are even here, Mr. Belle?"

"Of course not. This is a matter between men; nothing that concerns women."

Stuart returned to his chair, picked up his feet, and placed his boots on the far end of the table. "So, you think you can convince your sister-in-law not to return to Belle Mercantile and a job which she appears to thoroughly enjoy?"

"She can help out at home, supervising the servants."

Stuart chuckled.

"Sir," asked Belle, stepping toward the table again, "is there more to this incident that I should know?"

"No," said Stuart, shaking his head. "You know everything I know, and you have my pledge as a fellow gentleman." Stuart smiled. "Oh, that's right, I'm no gentleman." He gestured to the door. "Would you care to bring a notary aboard and have me sign a document? I hear you Belles are impressed with documents."

Denis did not care to and left, totally confused.

Two days later, Stuart took the *Mary Stewart* out and was gone for several months. When he returned, he went straight to Belle's Mercantile with a list of goods any good quartermaster could purchase. There, he saw Nelie assisting a customer. Stuart hung back, waiting for her to be free. Under his arm was a long box tied with twine.

"Oh, Captain Stuart," said the young woman with that cheery smile he'd so long missed, "I heard you have been to England. How was your trip?"

"Very productive." Stuart handed her the box. "Could you do me a favor, Miss Belle, and find someone to purchase this dress? I could ask one of the ladies who has a millinery shop, but . . ." Stuart glanced away. "I'm uncomfortable in those stores. They have more questions than I have answers."

Nelie's chuckle was music to the sailor's ears. "Oh, Captain Stuart, we need to find a wife for you, and she will buy all manner of garments and have box loads of reasons as to why she needs all those clothes. That's how a man learns the millinery trade."

"Miss Belle—"

"Please call me Nelie, Captain Stuart. You did before you sailed for London."

"I believe there were objections from some quarters about a pirate becoming too familiar with a lady."

"And I believe we have had this conversation before. It's you categorizing people, and you were never a pirate but a privateer."

"Miss Belle, I do not wish to offend."

"Oh, you mean the note that caused my brother-in-law to pay a call on your ship." Nelie nodded. "I understand, and the Belle family is indebted to you for what you have done."

"Miss Belle, I do not want your family to be in my debt. I simply want to go my way and your family to go theirs." And it broke Stuart's heart to say so.

Nelie was plainly surprised, but she was a master of customer relations. "Well, I certainly hope Stuart & Company will continue doing business with us."

"Of course. You have the best prices on the waterfront." He handed over the box, an oblong thing held together by string tied in both directions. "This might be something your store would like to offer, and my quartermaster can furnish the name of the wholesaler." Gesturing at the far side of the store, he added, "I notice you've knocked down the wall between you and the shop next door."

"A sign of the times," said Nelie, taking the box. "Charles Town is about to become more than a stop on the Atlantic Highway." But by the time Nelie had cut the string and opened the box, the Scot had disappeared out the door.

Inside the box was the latest fashion from Paris, and Nelie held up the bodice, snatching up the matching petticoat before it hit the floor. The jacket was rather bold, scooped low, close fitting to the waist, and flaring over the hips; sleeves just as tight and ending below the elbow. The frilled cuff of the chemise would emerge below the sleeve and the petticoat was cut to be worn over dome-shaped hoops. The silk fabric matched the blue of her eyes.

Nelie turned to the door and saw that Stuart was gone. It was all she could do not to rush outside and chase Stuart down the street. Returning to the mirror, she turned this way and that. Several male clerks glanced her way but displayed little interest in the dress.

One of the customers, a Goose Creek man, said, "If that's for sale, Miss Belle, wrap it up and I'll take it home. My wife likes such pretties."

But Nelie knew, as she clutched the dress tightly and looked at herself in the convex glass, that this dress would never be for sale.

Now, several months later, as the *Mary Stewart* sped toward the Outer Banks, Denis Belle made his way to the stern and asked for a moment of Stuart's time.

"Tell me, Mr. Belle," asked Stuart without turning around, "there were six letters sent to your sister-in-law while I was serving on the Main, but she never once referred to those letters, and your sister-in-law is a very gracious young woman, not to mention she always expresses an interest in my travels. Those letters took me many hours to compose and the bearer was promised an eight for delivery, an eight charged to my account six times by Belle Mercantile. What happened to those letters, sir?"

Belle appeared at a loss for words.

From behind him, Kyrle said, "An extinguished lantern on the poop deck means the captain doesn't wished to be disturbed."

"Oh," said Belle, glancing at the stern light. "My apologies, Captain Stuart, and when we return to Charles Town, I will make sure your account is adjusted for those six letters."

"No reason, Mr. Belle. I will never be beholden to you or your family."

"Now, Captain, there's no reason to quarrel."

Kyrle took Belle's arm. "Sir, you must leave this deck."

Belle looked from the extinguished light to the huge man with the white beard and the stocking cap.

"One moment, Mr. Kyrle," said Stuart, turning around.

The helmsman released the Frenchman's arm and moved away. "I'll be on the quarterdeck, Captain."

"You don't yield an inch, do you?" said Belle, once the Irishman had disappeared below.

"When I have, people like you have tried to run over me." Stuart looked up to where the red flag had fluttered. "For that reason, when we return to Charles Town, you might want to explain what a red flag means. It's all your wife needs to know about me, Mr. Belle."

FOURTEEN

The morning after the *Mary Stewart* sailed, Catherine Belle simply couldn't get out of bed. She just didn't see any reason, and last night it had been nigh impossible to get to sleep without several glasses of wine. At dinner, Uncle Antoine had repeatedly called her name to force her to concentrate on the loan he had requested for another gamecock. Finally, well after midnight, she had dropped off to sleep, but only after beginning to weep and without any good reason.

What did her uncle wish of her?

Whatever it was, it was entirely too much, and she didn't want to do it. She didn't want to do anything. But once her maid entered the room with her breakfast tray and pulled back the curtains, allowing the sunlight to splash across her face, Catherine sat up and allowed the maid to place a couple of pillows behind her back. Then she lay there, nibbling at a piece of toast and basking in the morning sunlight.

Still, it was quite a while before she could drag herself

out of bed, dress, and go into her office. Several of the clerks spoke to her as she crossed the sales floor, but she heard none of them.

It wasn't like she hadn't done all she could do to rescue Nelie. Really, once you gave someone a task, even a pirate hunter such as James Stuart, you assumed the work would be done.

Of course, when she'd taken over her uncle's store, she'd had to learn that the hard way. Running a business was all about . . . about what?

What?

Finding herself sitting behind the desk in her office, Catherine got up, closed the door, and proceeded to have a good cry. Finished, she dabbed at her eyes a final time, opened the door, and got down to business.

What had she been working on?

Oh, these past due accounts . . .

Moments later, she began to nod to herself.

Marriage to a pirate would rob Nelie of her naiveté, what little of it that might remain after being kidnapped. This could well turn out to be more traumatic than her father and brother being strung up along the road to Calais. Fortunately, Nelie had been asleep.

Or had she?

The head clerk came in with a stack of paperwork, and, as unobtrusively as possible, placed it on the corner of her desk.

Catherine glared at the stack, reached over, and knocked it to the floor, scattering papers everywhere. The thin man looked positively horrified as he picked up the paperwork, placed it in the seat of one of the visitor's chairs, and hurried out of the room.

Catherine glared at the open door. What did the man expect? Was she to do everything? Was everyone her responsibility?

She blinked and looked around. *Where was Nelie?*

The image flashed through her mind of her brother fighting to keep the noose from tightening around his neck, then tiring, and finally giving in to the noose, strangling and dying.

Uncle Antoine found her crying, and this time with the door open. He came around the desk and patted Catherine on the shoulder. "There, there, my dear. I'm sure Nelie will be home before you know it."

Catherine straightened her shoulders, sniffed, and touched a handkerchief to her eyes. "I'm fine, Uncle Antoine. Really, I am."

Her uncle did not remove his hand but began to rub her shoulder. "It came as quite a surprise that you even came in today. I was worried about you last night, my dear, and you retired so early."

An edge came into Catherine's voice as she said, "I'm behind on my accounts, and there's a layer of dust on the merchandise. I must be here to see that things are done properly."

Well, that was enough to douse whatever familial feelings Antoine had for his niece and he headed for the door. "I shall make sure that the layer of dust is removed immediately, my dear."

This he said rather stiffly, as Antoine Belle had never become comfortable with his niece's expectations, except at the end of the month when he and Denis checked the figures. Belle Mercantile was doing quite well, and for that reason, Antoine didn't believe anyone had to go around checking the employees' work. And if such checking must be done, it would certainly not be done by Antoine Belle.

Outside his niece's door, he passed a rough-looking customer by the name of Gaillard and Catherine's manservant, Caesar. Both men nodded, but Antoine did not return their acknowledgment. After all, you had to draw a line to whom you spoke. Then, once he had given the head clerk the order to remove that "layer of dust from the merchandise," he was off to conduct a bit of business of his own. With Denis out of town, Antoine felt he had a good chance of receiving a note with a favorable payment schedule, otherwise, how would he get back in the game?

It wasn't wine, women, or horse racing that had seduced Antoine Belle. Ever since arriving in Carolina, well, at least after viewing his first fight, Antoine had become an ardent fan of cockfighting, and when his last bird had been shredded, he'd had to go hat in hand to his niece for another stake—and had been turned down. His own son had sided with his wife, even when Antoine explained that he knew the location of a sure winner strutting around a barnyard on the Neck, not to mention, what would he do with that beautiful pair of silver spurs carefully crafted for a champion cock?

On his way to his lawyer's office, Antoine tapped his wallet and the paper it held. After reviewing these figures, who would have the nerve to turn him down?

Caesar knocked on the frame of the open door and announced that he and Mr. Gaillard had arrived. The customary procedure would have required Caesar and Gaillard to appear at the back door of the store, but it took so long for an employee to answer the rear door bell that Catherine simply told everyone to enter the building, walk down the hallway, and stand ready to be called into her presence. Her door was always open. People she was not expecting had to come through the entrance on East Bay.

From behind her desk, she gave Galliard a severe look. "Everything is as it should be?"

"Yes, ma'am." Gaillard smiled a tooth here and there, but mostly upper and lower gums. "The boat is ready, Mrs. Belle, and everything is set just as you asked."

"Very well." Catherine stood and came around the desk. "I'm putting my life in your hands, Mr. Gaillard."

More smiling and fewer teeth. "You can count on me, ma'am."

Catherine brought along a parasol and her purse, and as they passed through the retail side of the shop, she looked around for her uncle. He was nowhere to be seen. She asked Huger if he had seen her uncle.

The head clerk, a thin bird, stuck a finger in the collar of his shirt to loosen it, swallowed, and cleared his throat only to report that her uncle had just left the building.

"Did he mention where he was going?"

"Er—no, ma'am, he did not."

"Well," said Catherine, "that means you're in charge. I'll be upriver attending my cousin's funeral."

"Er—yes, ma'am," said Huger, nodding rapidly. "And may I extend my condolences. Will the store be closing?"

"Closing? Whatever for?"

Huger cleared his throat. "Well, your cousin—"

"Nonsense," said Catherine, sweeping out of the store. "Think of the sales that would be lost."

At the wharf, Gaillard assisted Catherine into a small boat fitted with a sail, and Caesar took the oars and rowed the craft into the middle of the harbor. Avoiding the larger ships by working the tiller, Caesar set sail up the Cooper.

On shore, two men in black suits approached Gaillard who had remained on the wharf. "Where is Mrs. Belle headed?" asked one of the men. "We had an appointment with her . . . her husband."

Gaillard looked from one man to the other. "You should know. You both have property up the Cooper."

The two men looked at each other, and then hurried down the bridge, climbed into a boat, and set sail up the Cooper.

A half hour later, Caesar said, "Miss Catherine, a boat is approaching from the stern, and it won't be much longer before they catch up with us."

Catherine was reclining on a cushion mounted on a board tilted at an angle. From beneath her parasol, she checked the shoreline and then twirled her parasol. The sun was climbing into the sky. Such a marvelous day to be alive. "Well, let's not disappoint them. Let them catch up with us."

After some ineffective tacking by Caesar, the two men in the other craft pulled alongside, struck their sail, and broke out the oars. Catherine asked Caesar to do the same, and the two boats moved upriver alongside each other; both being rowed.

"Mrs. Belle, we need to talk," said a square-shouldered man by the name of Fuller.

Catherine continued to recline, twirl her parasol, and watch puffs of clouds passing overhead. Shadows moved through the trees and undergrowth on one side of the river, but Catherine only glanced in their direction. Many people used the road to travel inland, but Catherine believed watercraft made for a much more pleasant way to travel.

"Oh, Mr. Fuller, you will want to speak with my uncle since my husband is out of town."

Fuller's companion maneuvered their boat closer so Fuller could take hold of Catherine's craft. When he did, Caesar pulled in his oars, as did Fuller's companion in the other boat. Since it was high tide, both crafts continued drifting upstream.

"Mrs. Belle, that speaking-with-your-husband might work with someone who's just gotten off the boat, but everyone knows you handle the Belles' affairs in Charles Town."

Catherine laughed and twirled her parasol. "Now that's the silliest thing I ever did hear. A woman running a business! Everyone knows we women don't have a head for figures."

"Mrs. Belle, I'm not the fool your husband is."

Catherine finally looked at the man. "Let me tell you what I do know, Mr. Fuller. Your family arrived on an earlier boat and you think we latecomers are to kowtow to you." Catherine addressed the man working the oars. "And, Mr. Mathews, I have met your wife and she shows little respect for the Belle family."

The man at the oars got to his feet. "Let me have a free hand with that woman. I'll teach her to respect what a man says."

Fuller let go of Catherine's boat to wave the oarsman back to his seat. Because of this, Caesar dipped his oars in the water and began to row again.

"Mrs. Belle, have your servant stop rowing!"

Catherine nodded to Caesar as she reclined on her cushioned board and trailed her hand in the water. Being outside was such a tonic!

"Mrs. Belle," said Fuller, once he had grasped the side of Catherine's boat again, "you have no idea what problems we have had with the Lords Proprietors before you arrived, and now that we're so close to having the Crown take over the colony, you make the governor feel much more important than he is, and with an arrogant man such as Johnson, that is the wrong play."

Catherine smiled sweetly. "The governor knows the Belle family is important. We are from Paris, after all."

"Mrs. Belle, you cannot act so highhanded."

"You are a stupid wench," said his oarsman, looking up and down the Cooper. "There's no one on these waters but us."

Catherine smiled at him. "If you think so, Mr. Mathews, why don't you have your way with me?"

Caesar gasped but said nothing. There was only one firearm on their boat and it was safely tucked away.

Mathews was standing again, but Fuller waved him back to his seat. "Mrs. Belle, why do you talk to us in this manner? If word gets out, everyone in Charles Town will shun you."

"Sir, everyone in Charles Town has already shunned my family, and as my husband will tell you, we are just trying to survive, as any family in this new world would do." With another twirl of her parasol, Catherine added, "Really, you should call on my husband and speak to him about this matter. I know how I'm treated by the other families in Charles Town, and that is the only matter which I, as a woman, am qualified to speak."

"Mrs. Belle, we have come to give you terms. Your prices on goods sold to the Indians must be raised, you must share what information François Belle has learned about rice cultivation at Cooper Hill, and your family must keep the governor at bay."

"The pirates," interjected the grumpy oarsman.

"Yes," said Fuller, nodding, "and you must stop dealing with pirates. That undercuts everyone."

"Well, as I said, I have no idea why you are speaking to me about such matters, but if you believe the Belle family will yield any advantage, my husband will soon dispel you of that."

The man at the oars smirked. "There's always the chance of fire at your place of business."

Catherine gestured at Caesar. "You realize, of course, my servant has just heard you threaten my family's livelihood."

Mathews laughed. "No African can present evidence at a trial of a white man."

"True," said Catherine, smiling slyly, "but remember your complaint: I have the ear of the governor."

His partner tried to quiet him.

Mathews would not be quieted. "We came out here to make this woman fall in line and present a united front to the governor, and here you are practically apologizing to her for our purposes. Dammit, she's just a woman."

"Yes," said Catherine, smiling again, "but a woman with resources."

The man at the oars snorted.

"Oh, but, Mr. Mathews, I understand more than you may think. From conversations with other wives, I learned that you are the third son, and that you did not inherit any land in Barbados, so you have come to Carolina to find someone you can lord over. Well, sir, it shall not be the Belle family."

"If you Frenchies didn't stick together . . ."

"So," said Catherine, smiling wickedly, "we are not all Carolinians, but you are English and I am French."

Mathews looked up at Fuller. "I will not be spoken to like this by some woman."

"And I say, sir, you are quite fortunate that my husband is not present or he would ask for satisfaction."

"Your husband . . . another French whore." To Fuller, the oarsman said, "I say we throw her and the African in the river and see if either of them can swim."

At that, Catherine closed her parasol, sat up, and whacked Fuller on the hand holding the two boats together. Fuller yelped, let go, and straightened up.

"Caesar, row for the middle of the river and hoist the sail." Catherine popped open her parasol in Fuller's face, making the square-shouldered man back off as he reached for her boat again.

The other boat rocked as the oarsman lunged for Catherine with both hands, palms open. "I'll show you—"

An arrow sliced through Mathews' hand. He gasped, straightened up, and found his other hand filled with another arrow. Both men looked for the source of the attack but saw only shadows in the trees and underbrush along the river.

"Indians!" they shouted and dropped to the bottom of their boat.

"Actually, members of the Lower Creek Nation," said Catherine, and she reclined again on her cushion while Caesar quickly hoisted the sail.

"Mrs. Belle," shouted Fuller, "you must get down!"

"Why?" called out Catherine. "The Belle family has never overcharged the Creeks, nor have we ever sold a member of their tribe into slavery to some sugar plantation in Barbados. Goodness gracious, what do you think the Yamassee War was all about?"

FIFTEEN

"**I** want to know what happened."

Catherine sat in the cabin at Cooper Hill on one of the benches made from the local pine. Other members of her family, especially Uncle Antoine, might think this place held little promise, but Catherine could see its potential. So could Uncle François, who was no one's uncle, but Huguenots did tend to stick together, as Mr. Mathews had pointed out. Not to mention François Belle knew Catherine would be instrumental in purchasing more land and more Africans to make Cooper Hill into something more than a one-cabin farm. That, too, was a point that François would argue. There was the main floor and the loft, where Marie and Nelie had slept, meaning two rooms, and the cabin had been built on raised fieldstones and had a plank floor with a huge brick chimney, a fireplace on the lower level. True, there were no glazed windows, but the family spent little time indoors.

Catherine saw none of this, only Marie dressed in a

white nightgown and lying on the table where the family took its meals. At her feet was a lamp.

Something had gone terribly wrong at Cooper Hill, and with the arrival of more Huguenots, especially those who were highly trained artisans, they could not afford to make the same mistake twice.

Catherine looked around. It was so dark in here with only the one lamp. Not a single window, but plenty of gun ports. The darkness made Catherine uneasy.

François gestured at the body on the table. "The girl was flighty and given to daydreaming. She thought she could be the next Anne Bonny."

François' sons stood near their father, heads bowed. They held their tongues while their father and this strange cousin of theirs discussed the death of the young woman who had been sent to live among them. Catherine was of their generation but spoke as an adult, and as an equal to their father.

"Who prepared the body?" asked Catherine.

"The female servants."

"The Africans?"

Catherine was shocked but determined not to show it. Why wasn't François familiar with other families along the Cooper? Any man living along this river should know other men, and one of those wives should have prepared Marie's body.

Well, at least no one had seen the bruising around Marie's neck. Such a waste. Several families had inquired as to the availability of Marie, but Catherine had turned them all down, saying Marie had duties at Cooper Hill. Besides, no one of prominence had asked for Marie's hand. That was the key to advancement in this new world, the same key as in the old one: the right connections.

The youngest of François' boys shifted around nervously.

Catherine focused her attention on him. "You have something to offer, Garin?"

The young man shook his head and stared at his boots.

"Perhaps you wish to return to the fields instead of attending your cousin's funeral?"

The young man's head jerked up. "No, no, I want to be here for Marie."

Garin was a lively boy, much like Nelie, and similarly given to flights of fancy. Catherine wondered if every family harbored at least one such fool.

A knock at the door intruded on her thoughts.

"Enter," said Catherine, raising her voice.

Caesar stuck his head in the cabin. "Miss Catherine, the pastor's boat has just made the turn."

"Then go down to the landing and bring his party ashore."

"Yes, ma'am."

Once the door closed, Catherine got to her feet and stepped over to her uncle and his sons. "It will not go well if the pastor learns Marie killed herself. He will not administer the sacraments." Catherine remembered the two men who had tried to assault her earlier in the day. "And it could become the sort of story that haunts our family for generations."

Catherine returned her attention to Garin. Forcing a smile, she asked, "Do you continue to court the Fuller girl?"

Garin only stared at his boots. None of the men said anything.

"Well? Are you still courting the girl?"

"Her parents . . ."

"What about her parents?"

François explained. "I have spoken to the girl's father—"

"And?"

"Fuller does not believe it's a favorable match."

"To marry a Belle? That's absurd."

Another knock at the door.

Everyone looked at the door.

"We'll revisit this issue later," said Catherine, "but it's time to bury your cousin. Everyone is to remember what I told you. If you cannot do as you were instructed, just burst into tears. It works for women."

The sons looked from their cousin to their father.

"If you do not follow your cousin's instructions," said François, "once the funeral has concluded, I will cut a sapling and explain everything once again."

The boys quickly nodded.

Catherine was at the door. "Well, is someone going to open this door for me?"

The men fell all over each other opening the door.

"Thank you."

The pastor and an altar boy stood on the stoop.

"Please come in," said Catherine, welcoming them into the cabin. "Everyone is upset over Marie's death, but she died as many others have before, defending Carolina from savages."

"Indians?" Very quickly the pastor and boy stepped inside. "There are Indians in these woods?"

"I was speaking of pirates." Catherine took the pastor's arm and led him over to where Marie lay on the table. The girl's face was pale, her golden brown hair pulled behind her head in a bun, and both eyes closed.

"Both Marie and Nelie fought for their lives. Marie was the unfortunate one. Her neck was broken in the struggle." Noticing the bruising, Catherine rushed on. "She hit the side of the boat kidnapping her. It's horrible. They threw Marie in the river like a piece of garbage. Uncle François had to fish her out." Shivering, Catherine added, "I just hope Captain Stuart is able to free my sister from that beast Blackbeard."

"There, there," said the pastor, patting Catherine's shoulder.

Though the white nightgown was buttoned tight around the neck, signs of excessive bruising were still evident. The pastor reached for the lamp at Marie's feet to examine the injury.

Catherine grasped his arm before he could pick up the lamp. Turning her head, she sobbed into his shoulder. "I can't stand to see Marie like this. What if . . . what if I have to bury my sister in a few days? I know it sounds horrible, but the sooner Marie is in her grave, the sooner I can put all this behind me."

So it wasn't long before Marie Belle was in the ground, buried under the very tree where she had hanged herself, the only way she could escape her dreary life at Cooper Hill.

After the pastor and the altar boy departed, Catherine rejoined Caesar in the boat and they sailed upriver.

In contrast to Cooper Hill's log cabin, the Fullers

owned a wood-framed home of two stories with plenty of glazed windows, and in addition to the numerous Africans toiling in the rice fields, one worked in a flowerbed lining the path up to the house.

Catherine shook her head in disgust. It was wrong to speak ill of the dead, but what had Marie been doing with her free time? No wonder the Fullers held the Belle family in such low esteem. Cooper Hill looked like the backwater farm that it was.

Then she understood.

What was needed at Cooper Hill was a woman who did not long to live in the city, and the Fuller family had three girls from which Garin could choose, and each girl had been raised in the country. Anyone of them would appreciate what the Belle family could do for her, not to mention demanding that more than another cabin be built at Cooper Hill.

And those indentured artisans on their way from London . . . They could be put to work immediately at Cooper Hill. As for the country house she dreamed of building, well, Catherine always carried plans for such a house—in her head.

A servant assisted Catherine ashore and then followed the white woman to the house, hurrying ahead of her and opening a door to the foyer. A startled Elizabeth Fuller met Catherine as she closed her parasol and entered the house

"Why, Catherine," she said, turning her puzzlement into a smile, "we had no idea you would be paying us a visit." Elizabeth took the younger woman's arm and gestured to the door. "Why don't you and I sit on the porch and have a lemonade?"

Catherine allowed herself to be ushered outside while the servant headed for the kitchen.

After taking a seat in one of the rockers and laying her parasol across her lap, Catherine asked, "Is your husband home?"

"Er—no," said Elizabeth, confused. "Why do you ask?"

"I thought he would've mentioned that I might call once my cousin was buried. I saw him and Mr. Mathews on the Cooper today." Catherine smiled. "And that fine boat of his."

"Well, that's just like a man." The older woman no longer smiled as she took her seat in the rocker. "We were sorry to hear of Marie's death."

"Thank you, but she is now at peace with our Lord."

The lemonades appeared, and after sipping from her glass, Catherine said, "Captain Stuart said he will not rest until he returns my sister to Charles Town and exacts a bounty from the pirates who killed Marie."

Elizabeth frowned. "Pirates killed Marie . . . but we heard—"

"Heard what?" Catherine used her free hand to make sure her parasol did not slip from her lap. What a fine thing it was to sit where you could watch the sun go down, far better than the dark and dank cabin at Cooper Hill.

"Oh," said Elizabeth, waving off the thought, "it's nothing."

"Please, Mrs. Fuller, I must know your thoughts on this matter. As you know, I am the female representative of the Belle family, and all things, even the most trivial, I must deal with."

"Well, of course," said Elizabeth, not knowing what else to say.

"Oh, speak your mind, Mrs. Fuller. I must hear the wisdom of other wives, especially those who arrived on earlier boats. Otherwise, how am I to guide my family in affairs of the heart?"

"Well," said Elizabeth, glancing away, "then you should know there was a nasty rumor that—"

"That what?"

"That Marie killed herself."

"Killed herself!" Catherine sat up so quickly she spilt her lemonade. The parasol slipped from her lap and clunked to the porch deck. "If that were so, the pastor would not have administered the sacraments."

Happily, Elizabeth Fuller saw her husband's boat docking at the landing. It would appear that he had taken Mathews home first. Still, he had been gone for an awfully long time.

A servant took the glass from Catherine and wiped it clean. But the white woman refused the lemonade when returned to her. Instead, Catherine had her fan out and was fanning vigorously. Much could be communicated if a woman had mastered the art of the fan.

"Still, we must look forward to more pleasant times," said Catherine, slowing the movement of her fan, "such as when your daughter and my cousin wed."

Elizabeth straightened up in her chair. "Mrs. Belle, you presume too much."

"Oh," said Catherine, surprised. The fan stopped. "I thought my uncle had spoken to your husband about this matter."

"He certainly has."

Catherine appeared puzzled, lazily moving the fan. "There was a conflict with the date?"

"Oh, no," said Elizabeth as she watched her husband hurry up the lane. "I'm sure there is no question about the matter."

"Elizabeth!" called her husband, now halfway to the house. "What are you doing outside?"

His wife didn't understand. She was sitting in a rocker on the very porch that her husband had insisted be built so he could sit and watch the sun go down over the river.

When Fuller reached the porch, he took his wife's arm. "Elizabeth, you must go inside immediately!"

Elizabeth still didn't understand, but she knew blood when she saw it, and there was blood on her husband's shirt. Allowing him to lift her from the rocker, she asked, "Have you been injured?"

Catherine remained in her chair while Fuller ushered his wife into the house.

"Arthur, what in the world is wrong?"

From inside, Catherine heard Fuller say, "You must never sit on that porch again. You and the girls are to remain in the house at all times."

Elizabeth thought her husband quite mad and said so. "Then what of Mrs. Belle? There she sits on your precious front porch with not a care in the world."

"I'm sure Mrs. Belle is quite safe out there."

"Safe? Safe from what? Safe from whom?"

Now the Fuller girls got into it with their father. They had been listening at the window of the downstairs parlor and wanted to know why they were to remain prisoners in their own home.

It was then that Catherine reentered the house. "If you don't mind, Mrs. Fuller, I will take my leave." Looking at the woman's husband, she said, "Mr. Fuller, I can guarantee the safety of your wife and girls on your property. They have nothing to fear."

Around him women had all manner of questions. Fuller ignored them all. "You can guarantee this?"

"Why, certainly," said Catherine, smiling. Now she looked at Fuller's daughter, the rather plain one who had won Garin's heart. "As I was saying to your wife before you arrived, once your Agnes and my cousin Garin are joined in marriage, you will feel even safer." Catherine stepped over and kissed Agnes Fuller on both cheeks. "Let me be the first to offer you and Garin best wishes."

Agnes became all aglow. "Is this so, Father? I'm to be wed?"

"What?" asked her father, confused.

"That I am betrothed to Garin?"

While the women twittered, Fuller glanced at the blood staining his shirt. "It's true, my dear. I have told Garin that he may call." Glancing at his wife, he added, "That is one of the reasons I was late."

And that was about all Elizabeth Fuller could stand, but her husband wasn't listening. He had taken the Belle woman by the arm and led her through the door, off the porch, and in the direction of the landing. Elizabeth was left to stand on the very porch where her husband said she could no longer sit, while her daughters remained in the foyer and complimented their sister on her choice of a beau. For someone who spent much of his time on a farm, Garin Belle was considered an excellent dancer.

As they walked toward the dock, Fuller said, "I have the blood of my neighbor on my shirt."

Catherine smiled up at him. "I'm sure you'll think of something, just as you did when you inferred that you and Mr. Mathews attended the funeral of my cousin today. Many things can happen along this river."

"You are assuring me that there will be no more attacks by the Lower Creeks."

"No more than they will attack anyone else. But I must tell you, Mr. Fuller, the Creeks are angry with the people of Charles Town."

"Indians have been angry before, and we have always beaten them back."

"Yes, and if I remember correctly, the last time their rage almost reached Charles Town. Yours was one of the families that took refuge there."

"The governor is encouraging the Cherokees to keep the Creeks busy. There doesn't appear to be any assistance coming from the Lords Proprietors."

At the dock, Catherine unhooked Fuller's arm from hers. "That may not be true. Word has reached me that funds were placed in a bank in Boston by the Lords Proprietors to purchase arms to be shipped to Charles Town."

"If that's true, then why couldn't the Proprietors send the money directly to the governor? No colony has suffered as Carolina has, not Virginia, not Pennsylvania, not Massachusetts. We desperately need to be a crown colony."

"Mr. Fuller, I have little understanding of the thinking of the Lords Proprietors, but I can tell you, after spending several afternoons at the Carolina Coffee

Shop in London, where the representative of the Lords Proprietors holds forth, we were told nothing but half-truths. That is the currency of the Lords Proprietors' realm."

Fuller studied her. "My neighbors and I may have misjudged you, Mrs. Belle."

"Sir, I am married to a gentleman and his father is a gentleman, neither suited for this new world. Truly, both of them remind me of why the Jamestown colony failed: too many gentlemen and not enough artisans."

Catherine gestured with her fan at the river. "I can understand why you and Mr. Mathews would not want to be seen negotiating with a woman, but I can assure you that the Belle family wants only to be a productive partner in the building of Charles Town. The proof is on the next ship. The new arrivals are excellent carpenters, and it would be a sad day if these latecomers were treated as shabbily as we have been, or forced into alliances, as the Belle family has been, with Indians or pirates."

SIXTEEN

Major Stede Bonnet was a father, husband, and successful Barbadian plantation owner. He was also a member of the island's militia when he purchased a sloop, renamed it the *Revenge*, outfitted her with cannon, hired a crew, and told his wife—a well-known shrew—that the new ship would be used in trade between the islands of the Caribbean and be absolutely safe from pirate attacks. But the moment the *Revenge* disappeared over the horizon, Bonnet hauled down the Union Jack and hoisted the Jolly Roger.

Bonnet was now a pirate captain, and before meeting Blackbeard, Bonnet had an incredible run of good luck, seizing ship after ship and providing his crew with plenty of rum, sugar, and slaves. With such a string of successes, several months passed before his crew realized Bonnet had no idea how to be a pirate captain. That's when Bonnet ran into Blackbeard, who recognized Bonnet for the novice he was. Blackbeard brought Bonnet aboard the *Queen Anne's Revenge* where he could study nautical charts and discuss strategy, while one of Blackbeard's men took charge of the *Revenge.*

Edward Teach, commonly called "Blackbeard" for his full black beard, a beard he filled with burning cannon fuses before boarding a ship, spent the winter seizing ships in the Caribbean and avoiding the heavily fortified islands of Jamaica and Cuba.

This had become Teach's pattern at the end of hostilities between Spain and England, or Queen Anne's War, seizing ships in the warmer waters of the Spanish Main before sailing north, where, during the summer, he plundered ships off the Atlantic Coast, thus becoming one of America's first snowbirds.

In 1718, that all changed.

Despite repeated assaults by the Spanish, French, and various Indian nations, Charles Town was beginning to live up to its potential, spilling over its defensive walls into the surrounding countryside, with palatial homes being built at White Point and more forest being turned into farms out on the Neck.

After all, any attack would come from the sea, but if an attack did originate inland, a skirmish line could be hastily formed across the Neck, the narrow piece of land between the Ashley and Cooper Rivers. What Charles Town wasn't expecting was a blockade, and when Blackbeard's ships appeared off Charles Town Bar, the harbormaster sailed out to assist these ships in navigating the Bar. His ship was the first to be boarded.

Charles Town was certainly worth plundering, with its elegant new homes belonging to the new mercantile elite, or those who could afford trips across the Atlantic. The day Blackbeard began his blockade, ten ships rode at anchorage in the harbor, all filled with a multitude of goods destined for the Caribbean, London, or the neighboring colonies, and when Blackbeard's fleet sailed away, Major Stede Bonnet, or "the gentleman pirate," as he became known, was vividly remembered by those held prisoner during the blockade, especially the ones sent ashore wearing only their drawers.

Again, Charles Town appealed to the Lords Proprietors for frigates and soldiers to defend their colony, but the viewpoint held in London was quite different: If these merchant princes were making so much money, why couldn't they finance, not only public improvements, but also the city's general defense?

Belle Mercantile and Stuart & Company would be two of those companies contributing little to the public coffers. Founded by former privateers and protected by British mercantile laws, Stuart & Company shipped all types of merchandise: hoops for barrel making, pitch, tar, beef, rice, candles, butter, and peas, and from the Spanish Main came rum, sugar, molasses, cotton, and salt. And since the leader of these former privateers remembered the example set by Sir Henry Morgan, profits were plowed back into the purchase and maintenance of more and more ships.

This take-it-for granted attitude was resented by those who had suffered through yellow fever epidemics and more than one Indian attack. In other words, the early settlers felt the same resentment toward Stuart & Company and the Belle family as the Lords Proprietors did against all the colonists in Carolina.

Colonel William Rhett was one of those who had beaten back attacks by the French, Spanish, and a variety of Indian tribes, and the day James Stuart set out to rescue Nelie Belle, the colonel appeared on Stuart's Bridge.

"Permission to come aboard," called Rhett from the bridge. William Rhett knew the courtesies of the sea. He had arrived in Charles Town with his own ship.

Stuart walked over to the gangway. "Please do so, Colonel, and we shall share a drink together."

But when Stuart headed for his cabin, Rhett hung back, watching the rum and whiskey destined for the hold of the *Mary Stewart.* One sailor handed off his keg to the next man in a line extending from carts on Stuart's Bridge, up the gangway, across the main deck, and down into the hold.

Policing the line were abstainers with French muskets, one posted on deck, another in the hold, and a third at the emptying cart. French muskets were the weapon of choice for pirates and privateers: a French long gun, lighter and more accurate than others, a true work of art.

"You don't trust your crew with its cargo?"

"Well, Colonel," said Stuart, "some of these men are not the most upstanding citizens of Charles Town."

"That's certainly true," said Rhett, chuckling. "I think you cleaned out the jail and the stocks."

Rhett saw Kyrle come aboard with several other

sailors as disheveled as the Irishman. Stuart flipped an eight to the constable accompanying them. The constable caught the coin, bit into it, and satisfied, saluted Stuart and disappeared down the gangway.

Watching the man go, Rhett said, "You seem to draw support from all quarters, Captain Stuart."

"As does anyone who trades in hard currency."

The four men accompanying Kyrle took their places in line and began passing kegs from Stuart's Bridge to the hold of the *Mary Stewart*. When one of them slowed the process by breathing deeply of a particular keg and sighing, Kyrle slapped him over the back of his head and the line began moving again. One of the men stacking kegs in the hold was Rodney Wickham.

Watching the carts emptying on Stuart's Bridge, Rhett said, "There might not be a keg of whisky or rum left in the whole city." He turned his attention to the Scot. "Governor Johnson has requested frigates and soldiers from the Lords Proprietors. When they arrive, I will go after Blackbeard. Will you sail with us?"

"I will."

Rhett pointed at the kegs. "Then what's this?"

"The ransom for the Belle girl."

The colonel looked into the hold, from which came the sound of hammering and sawing. "Quite a lot of ransom down there."

"Well, Blackbeard believes a drunken ship is a happy ship."

Rhett looked at Stuart, examining the remark for any sarcasm. There appeared to be none, so Rhett, who was known for his violent temper, listened to Stuart's explanation.

"Most of these spirits were paid for by merchants in this very harbor, some as far away as Goose Creek. Samuel Wragg had a hand in that. If Blackbeard's fleet remains intact, there could be upwards of five hundred men under his command. They could strike anywhere."

"You served with Teach?"

"With Captain Hornigold."

Rhett studied the Scot. "It's said not even Hornigold could decide which of you was the more vicious in the heat of battle."

"I have my own opinion, as would Teach." Stuart was amused at how thoroughly Edward Teach had duped everyone as to his true nature. Of course, if you didn't do as Teach demanded, you would either die or lose an important piece of your anatomy. Still, few seemed to know that Teach was well educated, came from an upstanding family in Bristol, and loved practical jokes. Robert Winder had been a part of one such joke, cruel as it was, when Teach had blown off the sailor's kneecap.

"Then you will wed Miss Belle?"

"If she'll have me."

"Even after she's spent considerable time with pirates?"

Stuart smiled and wondered how long it would be before he had to kill Rhett, or someone like him. "Colonel, I've spent most of my life with pirates, so I don't find them all that offensive."

He pointed to where Alexander was supervising the laying in of more cannon. "But if Teach or his men have harmed the girl, then you will have no need to sail. I will return with Blackbeard's head on the bow of the *Mary Stewart.*"

So, when the *Mary Stewart* arrived off Topsail Inlet, or Beaufort Inlet, as it is called nowadays, no one could believe what they saw. The *Queen Anne's Revenge* and the *Adventure* wallowed in the shallows, hung up on sandbars, bottoms split open, many of their stores washing back and forth in the tide.

Denis Belle joined Stuart at the railing. "What happened here?"

Stuart had his glass to his eye. "It would appear these ships have been abandoned." Stuart scanned the shoreline, a sandy harbor lined with palmettos and pines. A wide building with a low roof squatted on a low hill. "All I see is a bunch of pirates making for the tree line or sleeping on the beach. There's a hundred or more." Lowering his glass, he ordered, "Mr. Chase, turn out the crew."

"Hands 'bout ship!" shouted the quartermaster through a speaking trumpet. "Hands 'bout ship!"

Men poured onto the deck, carrying rifles, pistols, and cutlasses. The cabin boy stood by with a broadsword and a pistol for the captain. The boy found the pistol easy enough to handle, the broadsword quite another matter. Joining the cabin boy was another young man, his hands full of signal flags.

"Trim sails!" ordered Stuart.

When Chase gave this order, fifty men left their muskets and cutlasses on the main deck, leaped into the rigging, and climbed aloft. Soon all three sails of the *Mary Stewart* had been collected across their beams and the fifty sailors returned to the deck to reclaim their weapons.

"Man battle stations, Mr. Chase."

THE PIRATE AND THE BELLE

"Man battle stations!" shouted Chase fore and aft through the speaking trumpet. "Man battle stations!"

The crew reported to their battle stations while Alexander shouted orders across the main deck to the other group of cannoneers, then shouted similar orders through the hatch to the lower deck. The sailor with the best eye went aloft.

"Alexander, have a cannon sighted in on that building."

"Aye, aye, sir."

To the young man holding the flags, Stuart said, "Signal the other ships what we've found, and tell them to remain outside the harbor. Kyrle, take the *Mary Stewart* in."

"Aye, aye, sir."

Hearing this, the sailor in the rigging looked in the direction of a finger pier jutting into the harbor. "Distance to target four hundred yards." He hustled up the rigging toward the top, an unprotected platform on the mainmast.

Samuel Chase ordered two sailors to the bow, where they dropped lines and sounded depths on the starboard and larboard side, calling out numbers to the Irishman at the wheel. Chase posted himself next to Kyrle, as during any action, the place of the quartermaster was at the helm, the location of the brains and control of the ship.

"Sweepers, Mr. Chase."

At the quartermaster's command "Sweepers, to your oars," many of the topside sailors hustled to the lower deck and rowing oars appeared from gun ports on the lower deck. Rowing oars allowed the ship to make progress during calms or maneuver in tight spaces. Now the oars bit into the blue water and churned it white. Working in unison, the sweepers moved the *Mary Stewart* into Topsail Inlet.

"Alexander, focus cannons on the *Queen Anne's Revenge* and the *Adventure* until other targets appear. Mr. Chase, sharpshooters to the rigging and launch a longboat to inspect those two ships."

Once those orders were issued, Stuart shouted both fore and aft, "Everyone remain alert! Flanks become much closer once we enter any harbor."

Several "aye, ayes, sir," resounded, and cannons on both decks were loaded and wheeled into position. The young man Stuart had instructed to communicate with the other two ships began to run signals up the rigging.

Rodney Wickham was at sixes and sevens as to what to do. He was incapable of climbing rigging, not qualified to be part of any cannon crew, nor could he handle one of the long sweeper oars. Still, as he stood near the railing, surveying Topsail Inlet, a plan formed in his mind.

The ship's surgeon staggered over as the *Mary Stewart* passed, first the damaged *Queen Anne's Revenge* with its mainsail cracked, then the *Adventure*. The surgeon, a man with the face of a persistent drinker, leaned into the railing. "I've never seen anything like this before, except after a major naval engagement."

"No," said Stuart. "These ships were run aground."

"But both ships . . . ?"

"What would be especially odd would be if Israel Hands *were* handling the *Adventure* and unable to come to the assistance of the *Queen Anne's Revenge*."

From the lookout: "Distance to target three hundred yards."

Armed sailors went over the side and piled in beside those manning the oars, and soon a longboat headed for the *Queen Anne's Revenge*. One of those manning these shorter oars was Rodney Wickham who planned to desert the *Mary Stewart* and hide inside one of the abandoned ships.

Stuart said to the bosun, who had joined them at the railing: "Mr. Fitzwilliams, if you don't mind, take the longboat for an inspection of those two ships."

Fitzwilliams surveyed the beach and its increasing number of pirates. Onboard the *Mary Stewart*, everyone was tense, having no idea what to make of the situation. Pirates wandered out of the tree line, all heavily armed, each one holding a hand over his eyes to shade them from the sun. Stuart had brought the *Mary Stewart* into the inlet when the rising sun would be in the eyes of those onshore. Denis Belle, who stood next to him, had plenty of questions. Stuart told him to stand back and to shut up.

To the bosun, Stuart said, "A thorough inspection of both ships would be helpful, Mr. Fitzwilliams."

The cabin boy handed a pistol to the bosun, and Fitzwilliams reluctantly took the weapon and went over the side.

Members of the on-deck crew gripped their weapons or stood by their cannon, all scanning the harbor and trying to make sense of the scene that lay before them. It was possible that both ships had been careened, or beached, to clean, caulk, and repair their hulls, but this did not appear to be so.

A sloop lay at anchor, riding low in the water, but when the longboat from the *Mary Stewart* struck out for the *Queen Anne's Revenge,* nothing moved other than a few fishermen in their small boats. On the beach more pirates crept out of the palmettos and pines, and minutes later, Stuart upped his estimate to over two hundred men. Below deck, those manning the oars tried to peek though their rowing ports to see what was going on.

From the top: "Distance to pier two hundred yards." And, then, "Captain, there's another sloop at anchorage upriver."

Glasses swung in that direction, searching where the water disappeared into the tree line.

"Can you identify the vessel?" demanded Stuart.

None on deck could see what the lookout could see, and for that reason, spyglasses frantically reexamined the harbor, the fishermen, and the sloop riding low in the water, not to mention the hundreds of pirates.

"Cannot identify vessel," reported the lookout, "but there's no activity on deck. It flies no flag."

"Keep an eye," shouted Chase from the helm. He, too, had a glass rechecking the harbor.

To the cannon master, Stuart said, "Alexander, one array sighted in on the unknown ship, and bring Robert Winder to me."

"I'm here, Captain Stuart." The pirate limped over to the railing and pointed at the lone building overlooking the harbor. "That's Hammock House, so this—"

"What's that ship upriver, Winder? If you've brought my crew in harm's way . . ."

Winder shook his head. "No, no, Captain. I don't

know the sloop in the harbor, but I believe the upriver ship to be the *Revenge,* Major Bonnet's ship."

"Belle," said Stuart, lowering his glass, "make yourself useful. Keep an eye on this man."

"Yes, sir," said Denis, almost coming to attention. "I mean, aye, aye, sir." And he drew his sword from its scabbard.

"Now, there's no call for that," said Winder, stumbling away.

By the time the *Mary Stewart* dropped anchor, signals from the boat inspecting the *Queen Anne's Revenge* reported that the pirate ship had been abandoned. The longboat moved on to investigate the *Adventure,* and it was during the passage from the *Queen Anne's Revenge* to the *Adventure* that a young woman appeared at the door of Hammock House.

Sheltering her eyes from the sun, she stumbled out of the building and through the sand. A tall man followed her and took up a position near the door. He was dressed in black: a broad hat to block out the sun, breeches, waistcoat, frock coat, and knee boots. He sported a thick, black beard and carried a cane. Leather belts crossed his chest, and on those belts hung flintlocks. Daggers were stuck in his belt.

"Blackbeard," muttered Winder from where he stood beside Denis Belle. "The devil himself."

"Drop anchor," shouted Samuel Chase.

From overhead came a final call as the ship's anchor hit the water and the chain rattled along behind it. "Distance to target less than one hundred yards."

That was good, thought Stuart. Most marksmen couldn't hit a target at over one hundred yards. Stuart passed his telescope to the anxious Denis Belle, and everyone at the railing watched the young woman hold up the hem of her petticoats and hustle to the end of the pier where there appeared to be a makeshift shelter. The young woman wore no bonnet and her black hair made a striking contrast to her fair skin.

At the end of the pier, she stopped under its shelter and shouted, "James, is that you?"

Winder laughed. "Like I told you, Captain, it's the French whore Blackbeard plans to set up housekeeping with in Bath Town."

Without a word from Stuart, Kyrle picked up Winder and tossed him over the side.

SEVENTEEN

Denis Belle returned the glass to Stuart. "You did it, sir. You actually did it! You found my sister-in-law."

"Mr. Kyrle, take a boat, and two kegs and bring Miss Belle aboard."

"Aye, aye, sir."

Chase ordered a jolly boat to be lowered away and a keg of whiskey and rum to be brought topside. A medium-sized boat, the jolly boat was used for general-purpose work.

"Permission to go ashore," asked Belle, grinning from where he stood near the railing.

"Permission granted."

"Will you be going ashore, Captain?" asked Belle as Kyrle went over the side, a pistol in his belt, knife in its sheath, and climbing down the netting.

"No, sir. I remain in command of this ship."

"Ah, yes," said Belle, looking around. "I understand."

"That would be a first," muttered Stuart once the Frenchman had disappeared over the side.

Two kegs were lowered by netting to the jolly boat waiting below.

Samuel Chase was in charge of that, and he leaned over the railing and shouted, "Mr. Belle, you must arm yourself."

Standing beside the helmsman in the jolly boat, Denis looked from the quartermaster to his sister-in-law who continued to wave from the pier. On his hip, Belle wore his rapier. "Ah . . . yes."

"I've got it," said Alexander, dropping a pistol to Belle.

Now Stuart leaned over the side and said, "Mr. Kyrle, you are not to leave the boat, nor are you to allow Mr. Belle to return to the boat if he should abandon it. It matters little to me what Miss Belle will sacrifice by leaving behind any mementos of her stay at Topsail Inlet."

"Aye, aye, Captain."

"And, Mr. Belle," continued Stuart, gesturing with his head in the direction of the pier, "it's time you shouted to your sister-in-law to remain where she stands, not to leave the end of the pier."

Belle looked at the finger pier. He could not believe the number of pirates emerging from the tree line. There appeared to be hundreds, and quite a few had walked out to where Nelie stood. Denis realized it would be next to impossible for him to take the girl from the pier unless the pirates allowed him. Still, he formed his hands together, megaphone-like, and hollered for Nelie to remain where she stood.

The girl glanced behind her, saw all the pirates, and shouted, "I'm right here, Denis! I'll be right here!"

One of the pirates put his hand on Nelie's shoulder and shouted, "Aye, aye, Captain! She's right here."

Nelie tried to shrug off the hand, but the pirate held on tight.

On the *Mary Stewart*, Stuart said, "Have number one sharpshooter fire. The disrespectful pirate is the target—if that's not obvious."

Into the rigging, Chase shouted, "Number one rifle—fire!"

When Chase looked at the pier again, the pirate who had been holding onto Nelie's shoulder tumbled back, taking more than one of his mates with him to the pier. It didn't take long before the pier cleared of pirates, leaving Nelie and the dead man under the shelter. Nelie stepped away from the body, hand to her throat, and screamed.

Denis put his hands together again. "I'm on my way, Nelie! Stand fast! Stand fast! I'm on the way!"

"Stand fast?" asked Stuart, watching Kyrle pull on the oars of the jolly boat.

"Yes, sir," said Chase, grinning. "That Frenchie is a quick learner."

Stuart focused the glass on the entrance to Hammock House. When the pirate with his hand on Nelie's shoulder had been killed, Blackbeard had not moved but continued to lean on his cane and strike a pose.

Chase scanned the harbor with his glass. "How many do you count, Captain?"

"Four hundred, if there's a man."

Alexander drifted over to the railing separating the lower main deck from the upper quarterdeck. He looked up at them. "I've never seen this many pirates before."

"None of us has," said the ship's surgeon, "unless it was in a whorehouse in Nassau."

No one laughed. No one spoke. Everyone watched Denis Belle gather his sister-in-law in his arms and pull her off the pier. The girl appeared to resist but finally gave in and joined her brother-in-law in the boat.

"You see," said Stuart, nodding, "she wanted to return to Hammock House for her pretties."

Still, no one laughed, no one spoke, and everyone watched as Kyrle left the two kegs at the end of the pier, then put his back into his oars. In the bow of the jolly boat, Denis Belle consoled his sister-in-law who leaned into him, his arm around her shoulder. It wasn't long before the jolly boat returned to the *Mary Stewart*, following the longboat that had checked the condition of the *Adventure*.

The bosun came over the side, caught his breath, and made his report. "Nothing onboard either ship, Captain. Those ships ran aground and . . . and no one's made a start repairing them." He shook his head. "Shame, too. One of them was Dutch-built . . . well-constructed and fast."

The helmsman of the longboat listened but thought the report incomplete. He said, "There was a spy amongst us, sir. A stowaway who didn't return with the boat."

Few of the sailors heard either report. They were watching the pier collapse under the weight of all the pirates who had recognized the kegs for what they were and raced to the end of the pier. Soon the pirates were in the water, fighting over the kegs, or trying to keep from drowning, a couple of them sinking with the kegs.

The bosun shook his head at the sight. "No one does quality work any longer."

Again, Stuart checked Hammock House. Blackbeard had not moved. What the devil was he up to? Teach never did anything without cause.

Nelie knocked aside the glass and gave Stuart a big hug, then kissed him on the cheek. "I knew you'd come for me, James."

Denis followed her up the side of the ship, then straightened his shirt and breeches before joining them. He returned the pistol to Chase.

Nelie glanced at him. "And Denis. I knew you'd come for me, too." Looking bright and cheerful, the girl couldn't stop talking.

Many of the sailors openly stared at her, surely the most attractive woman any of them had seen lately. Her dress was mauve, and in the cutaway front her petticoats were yellow. On her feet were a pair of buckled shoes and her hair was pulled behind her head. Again she wore the Huguenot cross on her breast.

Nelie smiled, held Stuart's hand, and chattered on about how she'd never felt so safe as she did on this ship. Despite the chatter, she was, as Stuart noticed, as beautiful as ever, and he yearned to hold her. As of this date, he never had.

Words tumbled from her mouth. "I told Captain Teach that we were betrothed and that you would come for me. In that, I had the support of Major Bonnet."

Stuart looked at Denis Belle.

Belle didn't know what to say.

"Miss Belle," said the ship's surgeon, "perhaps you and I, and your brother-in-law, should retire to the captain's cabin?"

Nelie maintained a firm grip on Stuart's arm. "Oh, no. I belong to this man now."

Chase clapped Stuart on the back and congratulated him. So did Alexander and Kyrle, now that the Irishman had climbed aboard. Everyone congratulated the couple, Nelie smiling shyly and the sailors shaking Stuart's hand. The Scot tried to return the telescope to his eye but to no avail. Too many sailors wanted to clap him on the back or shake his hand.

Ignoring the frivolity, he asked, "Are we prepared to discharge the remaining kegs?"

"Aye, aye, sir," said Chase, still grinning, "but we must save one for the celebration of your engagement."

Kyrle removed his stocking cap and wiped his forehead. He stared at the shoreline. "I didn't know if those pirates were going to rush the boat or not."

"They did," said Alexander, joining in the laughter, "once you placed those kegs on the pier." He thumped the Irishman on the back. "First time I've ever seen you pass up a drink from an available keg."

Still in the water, the pirates fought over the kegs until one pirate succeeded in separating his fellows from one of the kegs and pushed it ashore. As he came out of the water and hoisted the keg to his shoulder, another pirate stepped forward and shot him. The other pirates weren't going to let the killer get away with that, and someone shot the killer in the back before he bent over to retrieve the keg. Soon, forty or fifty pirates were in the surf and fighting over this one keg.

"How many boats are available for unloading the remaining kegs?" Stuart felt the narrow cove closing in on him and his shoulders tightened. He wanted to put some blue water between him and those pirates. Still, Colonel Rhett would have questions, and he should have answers.

His quartermaster said, "Six longboats from each ship, along with a couple of smaller boats. But we'll take care of that, sir. You should spend some time with your fiancée. And, of course, Mr. Belle."

The ship's surgeon headed for Stuart's cabin. "Mr. Belle, please bring along your sister-in-law."

Nelie was puzzled by Stuart's lack of interest. Wasn't James happy to see her? Hadn't he missed her? And why did he continue to stare through that glass? She was safely aboard and standing beside him, not ashore.

"James . . . ?"

Stuart focused his glass on Blackbeard who smiled before ducking through the door of Hammock House, while, down at the shoreline, the pirates continued to fight over the two kegs.

Gesturing with his glass at the two ships run aground, Stuart asked the bosun: "Mr. Fitzwilliams, which of those two ships could you have up and running by the next high tide?"

The bosun studied the two ships, then glanced at the small board with the next high tide. "*Queen Anne's Revenge* is finished, Captain, but you give me a day and a bit and I'd have the *Adventure* ready to sail."

There was chatter all around, especially about the pirates fighting and killing each other in the surf. Unseen by anyone, Rodney Wickham struggled through the surf around the *Queen Anne's Revenge*, trying to find his footing in the unsure waters.

"Then," asked Stuart, still speaking with the bosun, "there's no serious damage to the *Adventure?*"

"I might have to steal a beam or two from *Queen Anne's Revenge,* but she'd be tight enough for blue water."

"And if I needed the *Adventure* to sail by morning?"

"Captain, you're not thinking—"

"I was only asking." Stuart turned the telescope over to his quartermaster. "I'm going ashore. Mr. Kyrle, we'll take your boat and two more kegs, one of each."

"Captain," said Chase, "there's no reason for that."

"James," said Nelie, gripping his arm, "please don't leave me. I couldn't stand it if you did."

"Take her to my cabin, Mr. Belle, and make sure she has anything she needs." To the ship's doctor, he said, "With all those kegs being unloaded, someone's sure to break a limb. Conclude your business with the Belles and return topside for duty."

"Of course, Captain."

"No, no, James," said Nelie when the ship's surgeon took her arm. "Don't do this!"

"I should accompany you ashore," said Denis Belle, his hand at his rapier.

"No, sir. You could be held for ransom."

"What about you?" cried Nelie as she was pulled toward the cabin. "What if Blackbeard won't let you leave? I'd just die . . . James, I'd just die." The girl collapsed in the surgeon's arms. "James, please don't do this. Please don't . . ."

But Stuart had disappeared over the side, down the netting, and into the jolly boat. Under Fitzwilliams' watchful eye, two kegs followed him over the side.

Once that was done, kegs began to appear from the hold and start their journey toward the railing. A couple of sailors sighed as the kegs passed through their hands and were then placed inside netting for lowering to the longboats and jolly boats. All hands had been promised a keg of their own, but Charles Town was a long way off, the sun was high in the sky, and they were thirsty now. That might be why the abstainers stood behind the men, their hands filled with pistols.

Alexander hollered to the boat below. "Avast, there, Captain! I'm coming with you." In his hand was a pistol and a red shirt.

"No," said Stuart, looking up. "Only Kyrle. How many cannons do you have trained on Hammock House?"

"As many as you wish." The cannon master wrapped the flintlock in the red shirt and dropped it to the boat.

"Well," said Stuart, catching them, "with your abilities, I'm sure it will take only one. Take us ashore, Mr. Kyrle."

The Irishman put his back into the oars, and Stuart pulled the red shirt over his grey one. The shirt matched the flag that flew from the mainmast, and, in truth, had been sewn from the same material.

As the boat headed toward shore, Chase continued to supervise the offloading of the kegs into the various boats from the *Mary Stewart,* joined by jolly boats and longboats from the other two ships, and some of the toughest-looking seamen who'd ever pulled an oar.

EIGHTEEN

Israel Hands, Blackbeard's quartermaster, met Stuart when he stepped ashore. Hands glanced at Stuart's helmsman, Kyrle, who wore, not only his knitted cap, but a pistol and sheathed dagger in his belt. Because the Irishman had balanced one keg on each shoulder, more than one pirate came down to the water and offered to carry the kegs up to Hammock House.

"Make way, people," said Stuart, a pistol in his hand, "and give Mr. Kyrle some room."

Despite their interest in the kegs, the pirates made a path through their ranks, which could only mean they recognized Stuart, or the capacity of the *Mary Stewart.*

Blackbeard's quartermaster ordered those in the surf to disband, then extended a hand to Stuart. "Good to see you again, Captain."

Stuart ignored the gesture. "Take me to see Teach."

Hands grinned. "Still the same old all-business James Stuart, eh?"

Hands stopped his grinning when he had to catch up with Kyrle and the Scot, and as they approached Hammock House, pirates closed in on all sides. Still, Hands wasn't quick enough to beat James Stuart through the door.

Inside, Blackbeard sat at a table, his back to the wall, in a corner of a common room. The innkeeper, a woman wearing a plain dress and apron, smiled from the other end of the low-ceilinged room. Stuart walked over to where he could take a seat next to Blackbeard, but with his back to the corner wall.

Once Kyrle placed a keg on the table, Stuart used his knife to open it, then pushed the keg over to the pirate. Placing the knife and his pistol on the table, Stuart took a seat. Blackbeard hoisted the keg over his shoulder and let the whiskey run out of the hole and into his mouth. When he had enough, he passed the keg to Stuart, who took a drink and passed the keg on to Hands and Kyrle. One by one, pirates entered the room and joined in emptying the keg, then turned their attention to the rum. When Blackbeard waved off the rum, the keg disappeared out the door.

Teach was half a foot taller than Stuart with a wild mat of black hair falling down his chest, and across his chest, a leather belt holding three flintlocks. His hair was braided in narrow plaits, each tied with a colorful ribbon. Daggers usually worn in his belt lay on the table in front of him.

"It's been a while, Stuart."

"It hasn't been long enough, but we can begin again once I take my leave."

Blackbeard laughed and glanced at Hands. "Still the same old business-as-usual Stuart."

"Aye, aye, that he is, Captain."

Stuart said, "You know Charles Town will be sending frigates and soldiers for you."

Blackbeard lost his smile. "Oh, they didn't send you?"

"Miss Belle is my fiancée."

"Is this true?" Teach appeared surprised. "I thought it might be some sort of ruse."

"It's the truth."

"Must be," said Blackbeard. "You always had trouble lying. Remember that time in New Providence when you, I, and Hornigold—"

"Perhaps another time, Teach."

"Very well." Blackbeard snapped his fingers, and the woman at the far end of the low-ceilinged room started in their direction. Blackbeard said, "I don't need any complications. I have enough of those already. I want you to know no one touched Miss Belle while she was with me. She was under my protection." The pirate captain spoke to the innkeeper. "Mrs. Andrews, if you please."

"Yes, sir, Captain Stuart," said the middle-aged woman, nodding more than necessary. "The captain said you'd be on your way and that I was to keep an eye out for your fiancée. Why, we even walked on the beach together."

"This is true," said Blackbeard. "I told your Nelie that she should say she was betrothed to me and that we would set up housekeeping in Bath Town, which, as you know, has been designated the official port of North Carolina by the Lords Proprietors. When she saw the sense in this, she agreed to act in public in such a manner, walking arm in arm and taking our meals together, but always with Mrs. Andrews in our company."

The innkeeper nodded again. "'Tis true, Captain Stuart. I was with your fiancée at all times. I even slept in her room."

Stuart looked at Blackbeard. "And for this, I'm not supposed to take offense."

"Take it anyway you want."

Straightening up in his seat, Stuart said, "Then I take offense at what you've done to the reputation of my fiancée."

Blackbeard raised an eyebrow. "So, shall we settle it now?"

"I wouldn't want to spoil your retirement, Teach, but take care that we don't cross paths again. Now, tell me, what's the ship upriver?"

"Oh, that's the *Revenge.* Belongs to a friend of mine."

"Then your friend had better watch his backside."

Blackbeard laughed again.

"So, Teach, what are you going to do about Charles Town? It won't wait for Virginia, it will want to exact its own revenge."

Blackbeard settled back in his seat. "Oh, those frigates the Lords Proprietors will send filled with soldiers. I'm not worried. Last time the Spanish and French almost overran Charles Town, the Lords Proprietors did nothing. It will be the same again."

"Colonel Rhett's very angry because of the blockade."

"Colonel Rhett, you say." Blackbeard smiled. "You

haven't caught him with his hand in the sugar barrel, have you?"

"I don't know what you're talking about."

"It takes a pirate to know another, and Rhett's just waiting his turn."

"I think Rhett means to make you his next turn."

Teach shook his head. "I have anticipated any move Virginia or South Carolina might make against me. I have a representative meeting with Governor Eden of North Carolina, and we shall be granted a pardon."

"And that representative is Stede Bonnet."

Blackbeard sat up. "How did you know . . . ?"

"Oh, please . . ." started Stuart.

The Scot was shaking his head when a wet Robert Winder was ushered into the room. Winder limped over to the table, and Kyrle got up from his seat and took a position against the wall. The innkeeper backed away, all the way across the low-ceilinged room.

"Well, well," said Winder, smiling, "if it's not my old captain. You're looking fit, Teach, but me, you can see the damage you've done."

Finding the whiskey keg empty and the rum keg missing, Winder fitted his bad leg under the table and took a seat opposite Stuart. He called for a drink. At the rear of the room, the innkeeper only wrung her hands.

"Sorry," said Teach, "no drink on this beach but for what Stuart has brought along, and you should be well acquainted with that." Blackbeard inclined his head toward Winder. "I take it he's the reason you were able to find me?"

Stuart said nothing.

"Why, Captain," said Winder, "they couldn't lash it out of me. Captain Stuart said he'd sail up and down the coast until he found you." Winder grinned. "And he did."

Blackbeard looked at Stuart.

Again, Stuart said nothing.

Teach took one of the pistols from the leather belt across his chest and cocked it. Both Hands and Kyrle put their hands on their weapons, but Stuart remained motionless. He didn't even reach for the knife in front of him.

When Blackbeard pointed his pistol at Stuart, the Scot asked, "You remember Alexander?"

Blackbeard nodded. "Uh-huh, and how many cannons does that African have aimed at Hammock House?"

Stuart smiled. "Enough."

At this, the innkeeper gasped and made herself scarce, Israel Hands went to stand at the door, and Kyrle pointed his pistol at Teach.

Blackbeard gestured at Stuart with his pistol. "I remember the trick about the red shirt and how everyone knows where you are during battle and your mates can't tell if you're wounded or not. What if I took that shirt and left Hammock House? Would that be enough to fool Alexander?"

"Not unless you shaved."

Blackbeard laughed, Winder laughed, and then Blackbeard turned the pistol on the injured pirate and pulled the trigger. The shot blew away most of Winder's face, and the lame pirate fell back, taking the chair to the floor. Israel Hands' pistol followed the dead man, but Kyrle's pistol remained pointed at Teach.

Blackbeard examined the man on the floor. "I guess you could say he outlived his usefulness." The pirate captain placed the expended pistol on top of Stuart's knife. "Now, let's get down to business. Since you didn't arrive cannons blasting, what did you bring to trade?"

"The hold of the *Mary Stewart* is full of one hundred kegs of rum and whiskey, and it's being offloaded as we speak."

At the mention of liquor, more pirates stuck their heads through the door.

"Enough for over four hundred men?" asked Blackbeard, skeptical.

Stuart pushed the discharged pistol aside and picked up his knife. "If you remember the size of your hold on the *Queen Anne's Revenge,* you know how many kegs the *Mary Stewart* carries. They're similar ships."

"Then I'm impressed. But you did always try to impress your betters."

"Teach," said Stuart, pushing back his chair and getting to his feet, "you should be impressed by Colonel Rhett. If the Lords Proprietors don't send those frigates, Rhett and Governor Johnson will put together a fleet and come looking for you."

Blackbeard laughed. "Then I shall pray for stormy weather. That's the only reason the French fleet was scattered during their last foray. It wasn't any of Colonel Rhett's doing." Blackbeard made a casual move with his hand. "But I intend to be pardoned. As I said, Stede Bonnet is with the governor as we speak."

"Who is this Stede Bonnet?" asked Stuart, returning his knife to its scabbard. "I keep hearing the name, but I don't know the man."

Blackbeard glanced at Winder, lying dead on the floor. "Someone else who has outlived his use . . ."

Rodney Wickham came charging through the door, racing across the room to lunge at Blackbeard, arms outstretched.

The pirate looked up and saw the young man headed in his direction. Teach fitted a foot on the chair between him and Wickham, and shoved it in the young man's path. Wickham tripped over the chair and went down, face first. When hauled to his feet by Israel Hands and another pirate, it was into the barrel of a pistol held by Blackbeard.

"Who are you, boy?"

"Rodney Wickham," said the young man, trying to break loose from the two pirates who held him.

"And your quarrel with me is?"

"You put . . ." His struggling was to no avail. "You put my mother in the hold of your ship. She almost suffocated to death."

Blackbeard leaned back in his chair, put the pistol on the table, and looked at Stuart, who had retaken his seat. "You know this boy?"

"Matter of fact, I do. I threw him off my ship in Charles Town."

"Well, you didn't throw him far enough." To the pirates holding Wickham, Blackbeard said, "Take him out to that pine with the odd limb and string him up."

"No," said Stuart, shaking his head. "Disembowel him, shoot him, or slit his throat, but don't string him up."

"And why is that?" asked Blackbeard, curious.

"Because Miss Belle will hear of it."

"And I care about that—why?"

"Her brother was strung up in France. Her father, too."

Blackbeard laughed. "You're a fool, Stuart. That's how I make my reputation." To the pirates, he said, "String him up so he suffocates to death like his mother almost did."

And Wickham was dragged from the room.

Stuart stood again. "You're a fool, Teach."

"Oh," said the pirate, looking up. "And why is that?"

"Because we might've gone our separate ways, but now I will certainly have to kill you."

Teach did not smile when he said, "Many have said that, and now they sleep in Davy Jones's locker."

"But none of those ever came at you with a broadsword."

Teach nodded very slowly. "Well, then, until that day."

As the Scot headed for the door, he was followed by Kyrle and a question from Blackbeard. "What will you tell Colonel Rhett when you return to Charles Town?"

At the doorway, Stuart faced the pirate again. "Just what you wanted me to tell him: that you've been pardoned by the governor and are living in Bath Town with a young French girl you've just made your wife." Stuart glanced at Winder lying on the floor. "Something Rhett could have gotten out of Winder if he'd found him first."

Blackbeard smiled. "But you're the one who found Winder."

"Or Winder found me. By the way, there's something you should know about the rum and whiskey."

Blackbeard straightened up in his chair. "Yes?"

The pirates at the door held their breaths.

"The kegs are being offloaded on the far side of the inlet."

Blackbeard was still laughing when Stuart and Kyrle left, and neither sailor saw another pirate, except for a couple of hundred backsides as the pirates sprinted for the far side of the harbor.

Outside Hammock House, Stuart looked up at the dead Wickham hanging from the pine tree. As Blackbeard had said, the pine did have an odd limb running out to one side.

"Cut him down," ordered Stuart.

The Irishman glanced at Hammock House.

"Don't worry about Teach. He's made his point."

Once Wickham was on the ground, his hands still gripping the rope around his neck, Stuart asked, "Dead or alive?"

Kyrle pulled out his knife, knelt down, and held the blade in front of the young man's mouth for a long moment. It never clouded up.

The Irishman looked up. "Dead, Captain."

Stuart had his pistol in his hand. "Then stand back."

Kyrle heaved his large frame off the ground and let the momentum carry him to his feet and away from the body. Once the helmsman was clear, Stuart fired a round into Wickham's chest.

Returning his knife to its sheath, Kyrle asked, "Why'd you do that, Captain?"

"So that when you return the boy to his mother, you can tell her that he died trying to kill Blackbeard."

NINETEEN

Once the three ships in his fleet had returned to sea, James Stuart joined Denis and Nelie Belle in his cabin. Nelie smiled as she filled his cup from a pot of tea the cook had prepared. All of them sat in chairs around the table, ignoring the noise from the quarterdeck, much of which were inquiries about the body of Rodney Wickham that had just been hauled aboard.

Nelie, it would appear, could not be distracted by the noise on the other side of the cabin door. "That was quite gallant of you to come to my rescue, Captain Stuart. A maiden could not ask for more."

The Scot accepted the tea with a smile. "The pleasure was all mine, Miss Belle."

Nelie had changed into a dress brought along in her brother-in-law's sea chest and had repaired the damage to her hair from her trip across the inlet in the jolly boat. Still, her face bore only a hint of red from her long hours in the sun.

After putting down the tea kettle, she took a seat on

the other side of the table opposite the two men. "But that doesn't mean you have to marry me."

Stuart almost choked on his tea.

Denis said, "Nelie, please . . ."

"If you don't mind, Denis, this discussion is between Captain Stuart and me."

Nelie smiled at Stuart, and when she did, it was hard for the former privateer to remember any of the difficulties of the previous days, even the previous hours. The girl was just so damn winsome, and that was the rub. As Nelie had done by sitting on the far side of the table, Stuart needed to put some distance between him and this young woman. He needed time to think, otherwise his resistance would disappear in those beautiful, blue eyes.

"Er—Miss Belle, may I make a suggestion?"

"Of course."

"If you don't mind, I would rather your brother-in-law put forth the concerns of those in Charles Town."

"Thank you, Captain Stuart . . ." started Denis Belle.

Nelie turned those blue eyes on her brother-in-law and the affect was completely different. "Denis, if you don't think I know that Captain Stuart has asked for my hand in marriage, you must take me for a fool."

"Nelie, really—"

"Why else would I have been sent to Cooper Hill? And if something's not done for Marie, and soon, well, frankly, I'm concerned for her sanity."

The two men glanced at each other, then Denis cleared his throat. "Nelie, I really don't know what you're talking about."

"Denis, if you aren't more forthcoming on this issue, this will become a very long trip back to Charles Town."

Belle looked at Stuart. No help there. The former pirate had settled into his chair and seemed to be enjoying Denis's predicament. "Very well, my dear. It's true. Catherine refused to allow you to marry below your station."

"What station?" asked Nelie with a laugh. "We were turned out of France, literally homeless, and now we find ourselves on the frontier of a new world. There are no stations, no positions in life. There is only survival." She inclined her head in the direction of the Scot. "Something we might learn a great deal about from Captain Stuart. He arrived in Carolina with only the shirt on his back."

"Nelie, you're not suggesting that the Belle family learn from pirates and other lowborn folk."

Nelie's warm smile fell on the Scot. "Captain Stuart, please do not take offense at what my brother-in-law says. He is quite the gentleman."

With her smile aimed at him, what else could Stuart do but agree with the girl.

"Now," said Nelie, patting down her petticoats, "since there doesn't appear to be anyone to represent my interest, I am forced to conclude that I must speak for myself. The question to be resolved is: are you prepared to make me your wife, Captain Stuart, or shall I look elsewhere for a husband?"

"Nelie," said Denis, "I represent your interest."

She ignored him. "And do not think my reputation has been soiled by this adventure and that you should take pity on me. All I have to do is return to Belle Mercantile and the men shall come calling."

"Nelie, you must not be so bold. It's not ladylike."

The young woman continued to ignore her brother-in-law, but it was becoming much more difficult for Stuart to ignore the sounds from the quarterdeck. He recognized those sounds. The crew had their blood lust up, and no one to take it out on. Neither Belle appeared to appreciate what was happening on the other side of the cabin door.

". . . only because I hinted at your attention that other men kept their distance." Nelie smiled. "You have quite a reputation along the waterfront, Captain Stuart." She looked into her lap and lowered her voice. "My brother-in-law thinks I speak too boldly, and what I say may sound too prideful, but I have been told on more than one occasion that I am considered a handsome woman."

Denis put down his teacup. "Nelie, I insist that you cease speaking in this manner. Captain Stuart, would you be so kind as to step outside while I have a private moment with my sister-in-law."

But Stuart was too stunned to speak, and his inaction only encouraged the girl.

"Shortly, there will be a good number of rich rice planters in South Carolina, and once the Lords Proprietors return the colony to the Crown, those who know how to turn rice into gold will dominate Charles Town society, not those who do so now."

Denis Belle was on his feet, moving around the table. "Nelie, this is not a proper conversation for a young lady to engage in with a young man. Captain Stuart, you must leave at once."

Stuart looked up at him. "But this is my cabin."

"Then we shall take a turn around the deck." Denis gripped Nelie's arm and pulled her from her chair.

Smiling as she was led away, Nelie said, "Well, James, it would appear that you must rescue me once again."

Her comment startled Stuart into sitting up. "Sir," he asked, "are you aware that there are over a hundred hands aboard this ship? Do you actually think you can hold a private conversation with so many men vying for your sister-in-law's attention?" And that was the polite way of saying what was happening on the other side of the door.

Denis ignored his warning and opened the cabin door.

On the quarterdeck, a sailor stumbled back from a blow, and another sailor moved in to finish him off. He did not get the chance. Samuel Chase laid him out with a belaying pin.

Seeing the Belles standing in the cabin door, their mouths hanging open, Chase smiled and said, "Sorry for the disturbance, Mr. Belle, Miss Belle, but some of the hands didn't have an opportunity to kill any pirates today and need to let off some steam."

Seeing that his attacker was down and out, the first sailor scrambled to his feet and went to kick the man laid out by the belaying pin.

"Thank you, Samuel," said the sailor, acknowledging Chase's effort.

Before the first sailor could swing his foot, Chase laid him out, too, and again apologized to the Belles.

Denis slammed shut the cabin door and faced Stuart

again. "No lady should be exposed to that. You must vacate your cabin immediately, Captain Stuart."

Still at the table, Stuart jerked a thumb over his shoulder at the crossed broadswords. "Sorry, but I'm in complete sympathy with those outside that door. Blackbeard was so reasonable today I never got a chance to bloody one of those things."

Denis glanced at the broadswords mounted on the wall. "You cannot be serious."

"As serious as the girl appears to be, and believe me, Mr. Belle, the hands would make a space for us on the main deck."

Nelie glanced at the swords and her chest filled with pride. Her hero was willing to duel for her.

"Mr. Belle, please consider that you and I may become brothers-in-law sometime in the future, and if I should kill you, your wife will never forgive me."

Belle straightened his shoulders and loosened his hold on Nelie. "I am afraid of no man."

"I know that." Stuart gestured at the girl with his teacup. "She's the one who frightens me."

Nelie was holding her arm out where she could see it, turning the arm this way and that. "I do wish you hadn't done that, Denis. You know how easily we Belle women bruise." Leaving her brother-in-law at the cabin door, she added, "Now, if you don't mind, I will conclude my negotiations with Captain Stuart." Nelie returned to the table and gestured at a chair across from the Scot. "With your permission, Captain."

"Of course," said Stuart, scrambling to his feet. And it didn't go unnoticed by the former privateer that the girl hadn't cried out when she'd been jerked from her chair. Nor did Nelie rub the place on her arm where her brother-in-law had grabbed her. She only examined where bruises might appear. What kind of girl was this?

Before Nelie took her seat, she said, "Please be seated, Captain Stuart. Would you like more tea?"

"No, no. I'm fine." But he wasn't. James Stuart was in way over his head.

After returning to his seat, Denis cleared his throat. "Nelie, may I ask how you know what you do about rice production? Our family eats rice, but I know few Englishmen who serve rice with their meals."

"Actually," said Nelie, after taking her chair, "the only complication is whether Carolina can produce a strain that will sell on the continent. If we can do that, then the East India Company, or some other company, will have parliament lift the commercial restrictions on the export of rice."

The two men stared at her.

Denis regained his senses first. "But that doesn't explain how you understand what you do about rice production."

"Why your wife talks of nothing else. Catherine's agents have instructions to outbid anyone for certain Africans at auction. Uncle Antoine complains of the prices paid for these Africans, but they come from what is called the Rice Coast of Africa, and they're teaching François and his sons how to cultivate rice." Nelie smiled at Stuart. "Marie will soon marry into one of those rich rice families, and the sooner, the better."

Again the two men glanced at each other but said nothing. In the silence, the sounds of scuffling and shouting came through the closed door. Those sounds did not appear to bother Nelie. She sipped from her tea and continued.

"Catherine says you tire easily of such discussions, and Uncle Antoine has little interest at all. At first I felt the same way, but Catherine called me a 'silly girl' once too often and dared me to find other silly girls in Charles Town. I found very few, that is, unless the young woman wished a man to consider her so."

She returned her attention to the man who had rescued her. "Captain Stuart, if I'd remained in France, I would've become a gentlewoman, but my sister and I were forced to emigrate, and though it took some time for me to understand, probably because I had my family looking out for my interest, I finally realized Charles Town is not Paris, not even Calais. Charles Town is a frontier town, and such towns require sturdy and dependable women. It is my children who will be raised as gentlemen and gentlewomen, and they shall return to England for their education while we original settlers build a city that shall forget its past."

TWENTY

"I was fortunate that Stede Bonnet was aboard the *Queen Anne's Revenge* to argue my case before Blackbeard. Major Bonnet said he had daughters of his own in Barbados and that he would not like to see me come to any harm. So if it were true that my fiancé was indeed James Stuart, he would come looking for me. Major Bonnet placed a chair in the stern and told me to take one of the lady's parasols left behind during the blockade and sit there. From that moment on, besides eating and sleeping, I was to do nothing but sit in the stern and watch for my fiancé."

Nelie sipped from her cup, and through the cabin door they heard Samuel Chase shouting orders for the crew to concentrate on the task at hand. With the continued noise from the quarterdeck, it didn't appear that he was very successful.

After returning the cup to its saucer, Nelie continued. "I did as Major Bonnet said, and soon he joined me for tea, as there could be no reasoning with Blackbeard. He and his henchmen had retired to his cabin and begun to drink. And I have to say I've never seen so many men drunk, and this drinking session did not end until there was a pistol shot and the injured Robert Winder was taken from Blackbeard's cabin, placed in a boat, and once a sail was mounted, pointed in the direction of Charles Town. The following day, I was thrown out of my chair by the accident of running aground—"

"Miss Belle, which ship ran aground first?"

Nelie looked at Stuart. "Why the *Queen Anne's Revenge.*"

"Did Israel Hands command the *Adventure* at that time?"

"He did."

"And what came of Hands' efforts to loosen the *Queen Anne's Revenge* from the sandbar?"

"The *Adventure* became hung up on another sandbar, and soon began to break apart, much like the *Queen Anne's Revenge.*"

Stuart leaned forward. "Was there any effort made to release the two ships from the sandbars after that?"

"Not that I know of, and I was on deck at all times."

Stuart leaned back and considered what she had said.

"Once we ran aground—"

"Please, Miss Belle. I'm trying to think."

"Of course."

Nelie got to her feet, went to the door, and summoned a new pot of tea from the cook. When Denis inquired as to how she felt, Nelie shook her head and inclined her head in the direction of Stuart. Denis glanced at the Scot who was staring off into space.

When a scream came from the other side of the cabin door, Stuart stood up, put down his teacup, and left the cabin. A half hour passed before he returned, and it didn't take a fool to appreciate why the noise level had been significantly reduced on the quarterdeck.

"I apologize for taking my leave without asking your permission, Miss Belle, but there were matters to make shipshape."

"I understand, sir, and do not think you have to consider my feelings when they conflict with the safety of the crew."

Stuart smiled before taking his seat. "You appear to have become acquainted with more than one concern of a ship's captain, Miss Belle."

"Well, sir, my life was in danger, and that has a way of sharpening one's senses."

Stuart didn't know what to make of this reply, and as incredible as it was to think of someone so attractive being that smart and articulate, when Nelie spoke, damn if she didn't sound like she could reason as well as any man. Not to mention there was no mean-spiritedness in her rejoinders, the signature of her older sister, Catherine.

"You mentioned South Carolina becoming a crown colony—when do you expect this to happen, Miss Belle?"

But Denis had heard enough. "Please, Captain Stuart, it distresses me to hear my sister-in-law speak of such matters."

"Sir, I did not ask your opinion."

"But don't you understand—"

"No, sir, I do not. I don't live in a world of subtleties and innuendoes."

Denis looked properly chagrin, nodded, and yielded the floor to his sister-in-law.

"Captain Stuart, you have more contacts in London than anyone I might know, perhaps even more than the governor, as your business is tied to commerce between the Crown and its colonies. Your guess as to when South Carolina will become a crown colony would be the more reliable one, not mine."

Nelie smiled. "Or are you asking how long you have to ask for my hand in marriage before one of those rich rice planters comes calling?"

"Pardon?" asked Denis, sitting up. What had the girl said?

Stuart returned Nelie's smile. "Is there anything you wish to tell me about your arrangements at Hammock House?"

"Sir," said Denis, rising from his chair, "please do not speak of my sister-in-law's accommodations while she was separated from her family. It is much too familiar."

Nelie waited for her brother-in-law to realize that his opinion had no place in the current discussion. Still, it was a few moments before Denis returned to his seat, and during this lull, few sounds came though the cabin door.

Nelie said to Stuart: "You, of course, spoke to Mrs. Andrews when you went ashore?"

"The innkeeper?"

"Yes."

"Er—yes, I did."

"Then why do you have these questions for me?"

Stuart blinked. It didn't appear there was any way

to get ahead of this girl in this conversation. Still, he would try. "There was one thing I noticed when looking through the glass from the *Mary Stewart*. It appeared that the shelter and the bench were newly built, whereas the pier had been there for sometime."

"Again the kindness of Major Bonnet. He had both the shelter and the bench built before he left to solicit Governor Eden for the pardon. During the day, the shelter was furnished with a keg of water, a cup, and several parasols. Major Bonnet was very kind to me and ordered his shipmates to remain off the pier, so I do hope he gains the pardon he so desperately desires."

Stuart watched Nelie sip her tea. He'd originally pegged her for a talker, but she appeared to have calmed down from the strain of earlier events of the day. "Miss Belle, I have another question, and bear in mind you spent a great deal of time under that shelter at the end of that pier . . ."

"Three long days," said Nelie, a sardonic smile crossing her face, "and me wearing dresses from clothing Blackbeard seized from the hostages during the blockade. I'm not sure I can face all those women when I return to Charles Town."

"Yes, yes, but what I would like to ask is whether you can see Governor Eden agreeing to such a pardon?"

"He would have no other choice. There were more than four hundred pirates at Topsail Inlet." Nelie paused before adding, "It's said Governor Spotswood doesn't allow any former pirate to remain in Virginia if he cannot demonstrate that he is usefully employed." Nelie touched her face which had remained pale during her long days in the sun. "I suppose you could say I was usefully employed under that shelter at the end of that pier. Still, my skin did not tan."

"Actually," said Stuart, leaving his chair and coming around the table, where he got down on one knee, "it appears to be the skin of just the sort of woman I wish to wed."

Stuart took Nelie's hand as Denis watched from his chair, half out of his seat. "Nelie Belle, I come before you as a former privateer and now ordinary seaman to ask for your hand in marriage."

Nelie's face scrunched up and tears began to roll down her cheeks.

When she tried to speak, Stuart gripped her hand and held up his other one. "Nelie, please don't speak. There are matters you must agree to if we are to be wed."

Nelie's chin trembled. She nodded and held her tongue. Still, the tears rolled, and she dabbed at them with a handkerchief from a pocket in her dress.

"I have three ships, a bridge, a house, and a warehouse, and there are mortgages on each."

Stuart glanced at Denis Belle before continuing. Nelie did not appear to notice. She was awash with tears, overcome by emotion, and gamely waving off her future husband's indebtedness.

"Then, there is my plan to relinquish my command of the *Mary Stewart*, enlarge my bridge and warehouse, and invest in an office where Samuel Chase and I can operate Stuart & Company. Charles Town has the best natural harbor between Havana and Boston. If we can learn to live in peace with Spain, our success will be assured."

Stuart cleared his throat. "But if this is true what you say about Cooper Hill becoming a successful rice plantation, you must understand that Stuart & Company will never invest in land but always turn our profits back into more ships, more warehouses, and a larger bridge. I operate in this manner because I received some excellent advice upon first arriving in Charles Town, advice passed down from Sir Henry Morgan. But that is of little importance. What I'm trying to explain is that you will never own a fine plantation home but will always live in a city house. And if we have any success, your world and your sister's world will grow farther apart, not closer."

Nelie's brow furrowed. "But there's no reason . . ."

Stuart looked to Denis Belle for assistance.

"Nelie, Captain Stuart is being quite honest in revealing the life the two of you might live together. You, yourself, have often complained of the rough nature and language of the seamen who patronize our store, and just outside that cabin door you had a sample of the world you are about to enter. All of this must be considered with any marriage proposal, and for a decent period of time I might add. What I'm saying, my dear, is do not turn a blind eye to the dream of those like your sister and myself who emigrated to Carolina to become country gentlemen and gentlewomen, whether we be French, Irish, or Scots."

Denis smiled down at Stuart, who remained on his knee. "Well, maybe not all Scots, but in the circles your sister and I travel, our friends came to America to acquire a country house with the accompanying leisure time to hunt, ride, and cultivate the mind. This, of course, is the legacy of the English King Charles and is not as warmly received by those in our own native land."

Stuart stared up into Nelie's blue eyes. "Still, my dear, you must understand that I would not allow the creation of such an enterprise to become an impediment to our happiness, but you must admit that you have been forewarned."

"Oh, James," said Nelie, enclosing his face with both hands, "you don't know how long I sat on that pier and waited—"

"Yes, my dear," said Stuart, nodding. "I understand."

"Oh, no, but you do not." She sat up, bringing his hands with her. "While I sat there, I reviewed what you would bring to our marriage and what I might contribute. Because of Stuart & Company's transactions with Belle Mercantile, I know a bit more about your business than you might think."

She glanced at her brother-in-law. "I'm sure my dowry will be adequate to pay off the mortgage on your house on Meeting Street, and we will have a home free and clear where we can raise our family. I would suggest, instead, that my dowry be used to enlarge your bridge and warehouse so you can remain ashore and solicit more business."

Again Nelie glanced at her brother-in-law. "You will certainly have all of the Belle family business from the moment we return to Charles Town, and you will be needed ashore . . ." Nelie flushed and looked away. ". . . not only to start a family, but also because Samuel Chase wishes to have his own command."

"No, my dear, upon that point you are wrong. Samuel wishes to join his wife in her bakery."

Nelie laughed. "I can assure you that Susannah Chase would rather have an indentured servant who will obey her orders, not a husband who will question them."

"But Samuel said . . ."

Nelie leaned over and kissed him on the lips. "You silly goose, do you really think Susannah wants a husband in her kitchen?"

Stuart did not know what to say. Only days ago he and Samuel had agreed that marriage complicated life for a sailor; now, this angel was telling him that, as a companion for life, she could be his helpmate. It wasn't the opinion a man often heard in the brothels of New Providence.

"James?" asked the angel, dropping her hands away from his face.

"I'm sorry," said Stuart, glancing at the cabin door. "I thought I heard someone call my name."

Nelie leaned over and kissed him again, this time rather tenderly. "Wrong again, my love. The only one who called your name was me."

Denis cleared his throat. "Nelie, please answer Captain Stuart's question."

Nelie straightened up and looked at her brother-in-law. "What question? I thought I was addressing his concerns."

"You've certainly addressed many of his concerns, but you haven't told Captain Stuart whether you would wed him or not."

TWENTY-ONE

Although not wanting to break his sister-in-law's buoyant mood, Denis determined this was the best time to tell her about the death of cousin Marie. At first, Nelie couldn't believe what she was hearing, and she made Denis explain more than once; not that that made much sense to her brother-in-law. The fool girl had hanged herself. It made quite a bit of sense to Nelie. If she had not gone to Cooper Hill, her cousin would still be alive. Perhaps Marie would have become a pirate, perhaps not, but she would be alive.

Her fiancé spent the night roaming the ship with his quartermaster. Most of the sailors were asleep in their hammocks slung below. Still, they found several drunk; not all that difficult because one of the sailors always sang when he was drinking and he had an inflated sense of his musical ability. Stuart seized the keg and threw it over the side.

"Clap them in irons," he ordered.

The liquor made the drunks brave, and they staggered after their captain.

Alexander appeared out of the darkness, both hands filled with pistols. "Come on, boys. I haven't had an opportunity to kill anyone all day."

Meekly, they allowed the cabin boy to harness them in chains. Stuart and Chase moved on to the grumbling of sailors in the throes of a major letdown, or what they believed was their proper due for making this trip: a sea battle with pirates.

Samuel Chase considered all of them fools. You have the opportunity to sail away with your prize, in this case, Nelie Belle, and you bemoan the missed opportunity to cross swords with over four hundred pirates. Chase had hoped he'd put all that behind him with the creation of Stuart & Company, but evidently not.

His captain's thoughts were elsewhere. Stuart knew he'd been away too long; actually, he'd left the cabin rather abruptly. But he didn't have the nerve to remain once Nelie had been informed of the death of her cousin.

As he'd gone out the door, he'd thrown over his shoulder, "This is a family matter."

"But, James," sobbed Nelie, "you will soon be family."

A little more than an hour later, Denis Belle fell in step with them. "It took a good deal of wine, but I finally got her to bed. Your bed, Captain, if you don't mind. The ship's surgeon had the cabin boy change the linen."

Stuart stopped and stared at the cabin door. "I think whatever makes her comfortable before we arrive in Charles Town is the order of the day. There, she'll have to run the gauntlet and be publicly and privately questioned about this whole affair. Lest we forget, it wasn't all that long ago that Nelie lost her family." Speaking to his future brother-in-law, he added, "Whatever you might think of me, sir, I've always kept that in mind. Tragedies such as hers are taken to the grave."

Denis's mind was otherwise occupied, gazing over the railing and out to sea. Suddenly, his head snapped around. "Captain, could one of your ships sail ahead and inform Charles Town that we are on our way and that Nelie is safe and sound?"

Stuart regarded him. "A grand entrance, is that what you want?"

"It's what the governor will want. What I want is for my sister-in-law to realize how concerned the citizens of Charles Town have been. I imagine all of Charles Town is probably tense. It's no different when one of the Indian nations is on the move: Mothers sleep with their children and husbands sleep with their rifles. If given enough time, I think the governor would have just about everyone in Charles Town at the harbor."

"I'm not sure I want Nelie subjected to all that."

"What choice do you have, Captain?" asked Chase. "As you said, anyone who walks in Belle Mercantile can question Nelie about her adventures. Who else but the governor to demand that her fellow Charlestonians allow Nelie to return to the routine of her former life? Someone from the government might even interview her and run off a broadsheet, answering all possible questions."

Stuart considered the proposal, then ordered one of the sailors to use signal lights and bring the other members of his fleet alongside. It took several hours and a severe reduction in canvas, but by dawn, one of the ships had pulled away from the other two.

Catherine Belle was at her desk when she heard the hooting and hollering out on the street, this, preceded by cannon fire. She didn't know what to make of it. She was reading a letter her lawyer had written informing her that her uncle had taken out a loan. When had Uncle Antoine done that?

The head clerk burst into her office. "It's one of Captain Stuart's ships sailing into the harbor, flags flying."

As if to punctuate his remarks, another cannon sounded.

Huger walked around the desk and offered his arm. "Mrs. Belle, may I have the honor of escorting you across the street to Stuart's Bridge. Your sister and husband are sure to be aboard."

Turned out they weren't.

That was just fine with the governor. It gave him a chance to gather a crowd, and by the time Johnson appeared at Stuart's Bridge, along with members of the Assembly and other self-important people, they lined the wharf four deep. Sketch artists took this opportunity to put together a portfolio to be sold in New York or Boston, where people read more than just the Bible. Lemonade was hawked; beer, too, and cooked meat and fish wrapped in bread. And since Charles Town considered itself an "open city," whores, gamblers, drunks, and pimps gathered with the regular folks, waiting for the second Stuart & Company ship to arrive. They did not have to wait long. The harbormaster led the second ship into the harbor, and once the Stuart & Company ship dropped anchor, a boat was lowered from the ship and rowed over.

The harbormaster turned his glass on the Charles Town Bar. "Where's the *Mary Stewart?*" he shouted to the jolly boat dispatched by the second Stuart & Company ship.

His only reply was a note. It read: Make way!

The *Mary Stewart* sailed toward Charles Town with Kyrle at the helm. In the Age of Sail, ships of any size had to be sailed, and Kyrle's seamanship surpassed everyone's onboard but James Stuart's. At the bow, sailors sounded readings, calling them back to the helm, and at the railing separating the deck from the helm, anxious faces looked up at the Irishman. One of those faces was the cannon master who shook his head, causing his black locks to flop around.

"Oh, you go to hell, you damn African!"

"Ready to do this, Mr. Kyrle?" asked Stuart.

"Aye, aye, sir."

"You are aware that my fiancée is aboard this ship."

Kyrle glanced at him. "I grew up on these waters, Captain. I know them like the back of my hand, and I sure as hell don't need no nursemaid."

Stuart put a hand on the larger man's shoulder. "Then give it a go, but bear in mind that no one remembers a grand gesture unless it fails."

Kyrle looked at the Scot, but not for long. The Charles Town Bar lay just ahead.

Denis and Nelie Belle stepped out of Stuart's cabin. Nelie waited for Denis to shut the door, then she took her brother-in-law's arm and crossed the deck to the helm. Denis saw they were approaching the harbor and immediately realized the *Mary Stewart* was passing the Bar, and without a leader.

Hurrying to the helm, he asked, "Where's the harbormaster?" His sister-in-law had to step lively to keep up with him.

Feigning innocence, Chase said, "Don't know, Mr. Belle. We signaled, but he never came out."

Continuing with the charade, Stuart said, "We've waited long enough to reunite Miss Belle with her sister." He gave a half bow to the young woman with the reddened eyes. "So, if you please, Miss Belle, I ordered Kyrle to take the *Mary Stewart* in."

Nelie appeared amused. "Is Mr. Kyrle anything like you when you sailed around Charles Town Harbor in your youth, Captain Stuart?"

Hands on the wheel, eyes straight ahead, the Irishman said, "Not at all, Miss Belle. I'm a much better sailor."

Stuart laughed.

"My apologies, Miss Belle," said Samuel Chase, "but it's common knowledge that you can't control what an Irishman says or how much he drinks."

Stuart's Bridge had hardly enough room for all the politicians, preachers, and poets who had gathered there for Nelie's return. One poet composed a poem in iambic pentameter about the heroic measures taken to rescue Nelie Belle from Blackbeard, and even before he had all the facts of the matter. Harpsichords, fiddles, and horns struck up songs, none of them the same tune; and several ladies had been pressed upon so much they almost fainted. Actually, the ones doing the pressing were pickpockets who moved on to their next mark.

Stumbling out of Carolina Tavern, a group of sailors crossed East Bay and attempted to force their way onto Stuart's Bridge. The governor was ready for that. The militia stood three deep where the wharf joined East Bay, and fighting quickly broke out as the sailors, rebuffed by the militia, turned their anger on any nearby townsman. No one appeared to notice that the ship entering the harbor flew the red flag.

No one but the governor, that is. Robert Johnson looked over the heads of those between him and East Bay and determined that if he was in danger from this ship flying the no-quarter flag, then everyone was doomed, packed like a deck of playing cards on Stuart's Bridge, and cannons loaded with celebrator rounds, not shot, per his instructions.

Chase double-checked the rigging as the *Mary Stewart* passed the Bar. "Captain, it would appear that we have failed to lower the red flag."

"Yes," said Stuart, without glancing up. "It would appear that we have."

Denis Belle edged over to Stuart. "I don't understand what you are doing, sir, and I would be less than honest if I didn't warn you that a marriage based on such unsure footing may not last."

"And you, sir," said Stuart, looking Belle in the eye,

"would know the truth of that statement more than any man in Charles Town."

Nelie, standing close enough to hear, laughed.

Denis attempted to rebuke Stuart, but Samuel Chase said, "If you could just give us a moment, Mr. Belle. This here's the tricky part."

Hearing that, Kyrle snorted, and Denis Belle returned to sweating at the rail. Sailors on the bow sounded readings and shouted them back to the helm, and those soundings varied sharply from shallow to deep, causing the *Mary Stewart* to weave this way and that with accompanying gasps from the crew when the ship scraped off corners of sandbars; all remembering Blackbeard's ships run aground at Topsail Inlet.

Kyrle only laughed and ordered a further reduction in sails. It would appear no one understood that the *Mary Stewart* was much lighter since discharging a hundred kegs of whiskey and rum at Topsail Inlet.

On Stuart's Bridge, Catherine turned to her clerk and asked, "Why didn't the harbormaster go out and lead them in?"

"I don't know," said Jacob Huger, "but I must say it doesn't appear safe."

When the crowd began to gather on the wharf, Antoine Belle had been on his way to a tavern where the cockpit was dug into the middle of the floor, the better for all to see. Now Antoine stood among those awaiting the return of his niece. Next to him stood Caesar, who carried a cage containing a new gamecock, and the servant held the cage on the far side of his body, away from Catherine Belle.

THE PIRATE AND THE BELLE

Uncle Antoine said, "There were over a hundred kegs of rum and whiskey on that ship. I'd imagine someone has gotten into the liquor and a disaster is at hand."

. That wasn't what Catherine wanted to hear, and she, like so many others on the wharf, glanced in the direction of East Bay.

Down front, a man wearing a tricorn hat shouted, "No, no, no!" And he began moving along the edge of the wharf and throwing his hands in the direction of Christ Church parish, or what would later become the future Mount Pleasant. Someone saw him coming, and when the man passed by, gave him a shove, sending the man flying into the harbor.

Laughter floated over the heads of those on the bridge, though the merriment distinctly fell away where it met the sound of a street brawl between sailors and the merchants who owned stores along East Bay. From under the merchants' black coats appeared staves of wood, and, one by one, the gamblers, pimps, drunks, and pickpockets were laid out. Pleased with their effort, the merchants tossed away their staves, shook hands, and smiled all around. It would appear there was a limit to what even an "open city" would tolerate. Then, at the very moment when the crowd was ready to bolt from the wharf, the oars appeared at the gun ports of the *Mary Stewart*, dug into the water, and slowed the ship to a stop.

When the *Mary Stewart* was finally moored at Stuart's Bridge and the gangplank lowered away, the governor rushed aboard. Behind him came the other members of the colonial government, leaving their fellow citizenry behind.

Catherine saw James Stuart standing on the quarterdeck and ordered her head clerk to bring Nelie to the upper deck. That would take some doing. Politicians were embracing Nelie and Denis, one so enthused that he embraced Kyrle, who was wiping his brow with his stocking cap. Uncle Antoine, seeing that his niece was safely home, took the cage from Caesar and slipped away with his new gamecock.

On deck, Alexander rushed to the wheel. "You damned Irishman, you could've gotten us all killed."

Kyrle scanned the main deck where the politicians clustered around Nelie and Denis Belle. "No great loss."

The governor took the hands of Denis and Nelie, walked them to the side of the ship, and holding their hands in his, raised everyone's hands overhead, producing shouts of joy from those on Stuart's Bridge and those lining East Bay. In the last few years, the residents of Charles Town had had little to celebrate, and this came as a welcome release.

With Huger's assistance, Catherine finally worked her way up the gangplank, but was shoved aside by those who wanted to greet her sister. Finally, she dismissed her head clerk, gathered her petticoats, and climbed to the quarterdeck, joining James Stuart.

After opening her parasol, she inclined her head toward the main deck. "You don't want your day in the sun, Captain Stuart?"

The former privateer smiled and said, "No, Mrs. Belle. All I want is your sister."

TWENTY-TWO

Catherine took an envelope from her purse and handed it to Stuart. "This is for the safe return of my sister. You no longer have a mortgage on the *Mary Stewart.*"

Stuart shook his head. "I didn't do this for you or your family. I did it for Nelie."

"Take it, Captain Stuart. I know what it's like to lose a mother." Catherine held the envelope out a second time, and when Stuart refused it again, she returned the envelope to her purse.

"Very well. Continue to make payments to my attorney." With no banks in Charles Town, lawyers handled all the money.

Catherine strolled to the railing where she could overlook the main deck where dignitaries surrounded her sister. Before she spoke again, she gauged the distance between her and the sailors on the quarterdeck.

"You will still marry the girl," asked Catherine, "after all she's been through?"

"You know, Mrs. Belle," said Stuart, joining her at the rail, "you two sisters could not be more different."

"You are absolutely correct. Nelie is a silly girl."

"I don't think—"

"Oh, this is such a tiresome conversation." Catherine lowered her voice. "I'm only holding it with you because you might make a *faux pas*. You can't navigate Charles Town as you do the Outer Banks, Captain Stuart."

She snapped open her parasol and mounted it on her shoulder. On the main deck below them, sailors lounged against the railing and watched the politicians buss her sister.

"You jumped ship in this harbor, and when you were old enough to sail the Spanish Main, you were clever enough to take the king's pardon and return to Charles Town, along with the riff-raff that seems to follow you everywhere you go."

"They follow me out of loyalty, Mrs. Belle. Something you will always have to purchase. Still, you make my accomplishments appear as if I disposed of my duties quite adequately."

"Of that there is no dispute. That's why I picked your ship on which to purchase a mortgage. The other parts and parcels of your property were icing on the cake. It was you I wanted to rescue my sister, not Colonel Rhett. He might've gotten my sister killed, a man much too eager to use his cannons."

Her remark caused a tremor to run though Stuart. That's what I might've done, thought Stuart, until I was stopped on the street by Samuel Wragg's attorney who suggested another avenue of approach: one hundred kegs of whiskey and rum.

The Belle woman was talking. He should be listening.

". . . admit I was falling apart. I think you saw a bit of that the day I arrived at your house without a chaperone, and later, at the office, when I did all that silly crying."

Stuart could only stare at the woman.

Catherine glanced at him. "The day after you departed, I took to bed, and Dr. Rose would not allow me to return to work until today. That's why I was able to meet your ship. Otherwise, you would've found me in my bedchamber with the draperies pulled and my maid threatening anyone with the lash if they were the least bit noisy."

That was enough for Stuart to find his voice. "I'm sorry, Mrs. Belle, but I find this all difficult to believe. You've always struck me as a rather strong woman."

"Believe what you wish, but if Nelie and Denis had failed to return, what would I have had to live for?"

Stuart didn't know what to say to that. Until this point, he'd been consumed with the pursuit of this woman's younger sister, but now he'd have to reevaluate his world, with an eye toward what impact on that world this older sister would have.

"I had no idea you cared so much about your family, and I'm not sure that you really do. I think they're a means to an end."

"Oh, you think just like a man," said Catherine, twirling her parasol on her shoulder. "Everything wrapped into one package. Issues are much more complicated for me." Lowering her voice so that the sailors on the quarterdeck could not hear, she said, "I left a baby brother in France."

"I don't understand. Nelie told me you, she, and the baby escaped through the bottom of your family's carriage."

"We did, and the family that took us in, after we'd wandered the countryside for several days, were farmers with no children of their own. That was the bargain I struck: my baby brother for safe passage for me and Nelie to Calais."

She saw the stunned look on Stuart's face. "What was I to do? I was fifteen, my baby brother was still nursing, and I had to get Nelie out of France."

"So, these farmers are raising your brother?"

"A brother I shall probably never see again."

"And this family protected you and your sister from the *dragonnades.*"

"That they did, Captain Stuart."

"But to do that they would've had to have been Catholics."

Catherine said nothing, only stared down at the main deck where the celebration appeared to be breaking up.

"But why do you continue to run Belle Mercantile when you could live the life of a gentlewoman?"

Catherine glanced around the quarterdeck where sailors performed their final duties. "Please watch your tongue, Captain Stuart. But to answer your question, do you think I actually want to be burdened with these responsibilities? Denis is at a loss when it comes to business, as is my uncle. They were both raised as gentlemen and don't know the value of a pound."

Lowering her voice even more, and leaning toward Stuart, she added, "When they escaped from Paris, word was left with my father that we could join them, but upon our arrival, I learned Uncle Antoine had purchased a shop for much more than the value of its current stock. Worse, when the store was restocked, many of the expensive items sprouted legs and walked out the front door. The last in a series of unpleasant occurrences was when the head clerk ran off with the receipts. Not that there were that many receipts, but his actions put Belle Mercantile into bankruptcy, and I don't care for debtor's prison or to be put in service as someone's maid."

"I'm sure it didn't help that you were a woman."

"*Au contraire,*" said Catherine, a sly smile crossing her face. "Being a woman was what saved Belle Mercantile, and I do believe you pirates, at least the ones I dealt with to undercut my competition, had never dealt with a gentlewoman, judging by the way they fell all over themselves to cut the best bargain."

Catherine watched her sister and husband speaking to the last of the dignitaries on the deck below, one of them a scribe taking notes with a quill, ink bottle, and sheet of paper.

Samuel Chase had posted guards at the upper and lower gangway. Now the doors to the warehouse on Stuart's Bridge were thrown open so the *Mary Stewart* could reload, this time with a regular shipment for England or one of the other colonies. Sailors trooped down the gangway and into the warehouse, but far more of them slipped away, having gone much too long between drinks, or a good fight. There would be a good many fights later in the day, and sailors along the waterfront knew it wouldn't take long to find one.

Catherine gestured at Middle Bridge, the largest wharf in the harbor. "You could've had a bridge that size by now if you'd married the right woman."

"I had hoped your sister would be that woman."

"What utter nonsense!" Catherine spun her parasol again as it rode on her shoulder. "Whether you'll fit into our circle is still open to debate. Still, your house has enough room to ground Nelie in the responsibilities of marriage." Catherine tilted her head. "When Denis and I move to Cooper Hill, you may lease our home from me, well, from us."

"Who says I want—"

"Oh, who cares where you live! The true test comes in whether you are able to climb the ladder. It always comes back to the ladder."

"Ladder?" asked Stuart, glancing toward the main deck below. "What ladder?"

"The social ladder, of course. Up to this time, you've had no roots, and it mattered little because the only family you knew was a bunch of cutthroats. The question is whether you can become a productive member of society with the martial duties you are about to assume. In a few years, Charles Town will change as you've never imagined."

Denis looked up from the main deck and smiled.

Catherine returned his smile. "That's why I married Denis. I plan to have a gentleman living with me at Cooper Hill." Before gathering her petticoats and going down to the main deck, Catherine once again gestured at the harbor. "I leave all this to you and my sister."

"Your sister says there are no gentlemen or gentlewomen in Charles Town."

From the other side of the railing, Catherine looked up at him. "In that case, Nelie would be wrong, and I shall have great fun proving that to her since she is betrothed to a pirate." And down the ladder she went.

Catherine let her husband give her a peck on the cheek, but when she went to embrace Nelie, she found her sister holding hands with James Stuart. Somehow the pirate had beaten her to the main deck.

Though Nelie appeared fatigued, her face glowed as she held the hand of her fiancé. "There were so many people . . ."

Denis wasn't finished with his wife. He put his arms around her. "So happy to see you, darling."

Catherine pushed Denis back where she could see him but remain in his arms. "And I'm pleased to see you safely home, husband."

"I have so much to tell you."

"Save it for the dinner table." She glanced at the sailors trooping down the gangway. "It appears we can go ashore."

Denis bowed to Stuart and said he would send Caesar for his sea chest. "Thank you again, Captain Stuart. The Belle family will always be in your debt." He took his wife's arm, and once the gangway cleared, they walked down to Stuart's Bridge. Whispering in her ear, Denis said, "Regarding the stories I might have to tell, I think they are more appropriate for the boudoir."

At the foot of the gangway, Catherine pulled away. "Really, Denis, consider how you speak to me in public. If you wish to scream at me at home, that is your due as a husband, but I must point out that you have always enjoyed the stimulating conversation of our dinner table."

"Ah," said Denis, smiling, "but after my adventures, that might not be the type of stimulation I desire."

TWENTY-THREE

Denis and Catherine Belle walked away, heads together, but once they reached the foot of the gangway, Caesar, who had driven their carriage onto the bridge, pointed at the couple remaining on deck. Catherine and Denis turned around and saw Nelie and James, chatting away. Catherine jabbed an elbow into her husband's side.

After catching his breath, Denis called, "Nelie!"

"Off in their own little world," commented Stuart from where they stood near the railing.

"Yes," said Nelie, puzzled, "but in what world? I've seen them whisper in public or revert to French, but hardly do I ever see them walking arm in arm. They act like when they were first married."

"Oh," said Stuart, smiling, "someone stealing your moment?"

"You know, that just may be it." Nelie waved to her brother-in-law and her sister. "Coming!"

Heading down the gangway, Stuart gestured at

Middle Bridge. "Your sister said I could've had a larger bridge and warehouse if I'd married earlier."

"Wrong," said Nelie, tightening her grip on his arm. "You would be dead."

At the bottom of the gangway, the Belles were joined by Colonel Rhett who doffed his hat and introduced himself to the two women. Denis gave him a half-bow. Rhett didn't know what to do with that so he nodded and returned his hat to his head.

"A moment of your time, Captain Stuart. I wanted to return once all the festivities concluded and ask a few questions."

"Do these questions refer to Topsail Inlet?"

"Of course. You know the lay of the land, so to speak."

Stuart called to his quartermaster standing at the head of the gangway. Chase was overseeing the netting of cargo from the warehouse on the bridge to the hold of the *Mary Stewart.*

"Samuel, would you make the colonel comfortable? I'll be right there."

"Aye, aye, sir."

Again, Rhett doffed his hat before heading up the gangway.

"You know," mused Denis Belle, "I must learn not to bow."

"And the sooner the better," snapped his wife.

Stuart and Denis watched Rhett stride up the gangway, then the two men looked at each other, then Nelie. Caesar stood ready with the carriage door open.

This caused Catherine to ask her husband, "What are we waiting for?"

Denis ignored her. "You think Nelie should remain here, don't you?"

Stuart nodded.

Catherine didn't understand.

"My dear, Colonel Rhett simply wants to know the disposition of Blackbeard's men at Topsail Inlet."

"Very well. Nelie and I shall meet you at home. Come along, Nelie."

"My dear, you misunderstood. Nelie needs to attend this meeting."

"I rather think not. My sister has been exposed to too much crudity in the last few days. She will not be discussing preparations for a naval engagement." Catherine reached for Nelie's hand and found it occupied by Nelie's fiancé. "Captain Stuart, public displays of affection are frowned upon in this family."

Stuart dropped his fiancée's hand, but Nelie quickly grabbed it again. Stuart looked at her.

So did her sister. "Nelie, if you want to cheapen yourself in public, I would prefer that you do it once you have left my home."

"Our home," whispered Denis.

"What?" asked Catherine, puzzled.

"Mrs. Belle," said Stuart, "what Colonel Rhett wishes to discuss is no light matter. He is about to take a good number of Carolinians in harm's way, and any information Nelie can provide might make a difference in the number of lives saved."

"But you were there. You can provide all the information Colonel Rhett requires."

"I used a glass. I was not ashore."

"Catherine, we are all family—" started her husband.

"I hardly think so and possibly not at all!" And after being assisted into the carriage by Caesar, she slammed shut the door.

Once Caesar wheeled the vehicle around and left the bridge, Denis said, "Well, there goes more than dinner."

A few minutes later, Colonel Rhett stormed off the *Mary Stewart*. On Stuart's Bridge, he shook his fist at those on deck. "You will hear more about this, Captain Stuart." Rhett scanned the wharf where nets filled with goods were being swung aboard the *Mary Stewart*. "And you may as well shutter your establishment for I doubt anyone will be doing much business with you pirates in the future."

Stuart turned to his quartermaster. "Samuel, if we're to continue living in this town, we need to reach the governor before Rhett poisons the well."

"I have a carriage ready and waiting, Captain."

"Then do it."

Stuart offered his arm to his fiancée and down the gangway they went, followed by Denis Belle. Behind them, Chase waved the red flag overhead and followed the other three to the bridge.

Colonel Rhett tried to hail the same carriage, but the driver drove to the end of the bridge and wheeled the vehicle around. When it stopped at the foot of the gangway, Stuart opened the door and Nelie climbed inside. She was followed by Stuart, Chase, and Denis who promised the driver a piece of eight if he could reach the governor's office before the man on foot beat them there.

The eight paid off, and the three of them entered the governor's reception room well before Colonel Rhett, Samuel Chase having been dropped off along the way.

The governor's secretary, a small, balding man, looked up from his desk. "Would you state the nature of your business?"

Nelie flashed a radiant smile. "Were you not there to welcome me home? I really don't remember. There were so many people." She gave a modified curtsey, restricted by the stays of her corset. "I'm Nelie Belle."

"Oh, Miss Belle," said the secretary, putting down his quill and hustling to his feet. "I didn't recognize you. I'm sorry I couldn't attend the festivities, but you look fit as a fiddle."

"And your name, sir, if I may ask?"

"Nehemiah Hovey."

Nelie gestured at the two men behind her. "Mr. Hovey, this is my brother-in-law, Denis Belle, and my fiancé, James Stuart." Blushing, Nelie added, "We are just now engaged."

Hovey reached across the desk and shook both men's hands. To Stuart, he said, "Congratulations, sir."

Samuel Chase came through the door carrying two baskets. "Sorry I'm late." He crossed the room, placed one of the baskets on the desk, and when the quartermaster pulled back the cloth, the governor's secretary could see that the basket was filled with sticky buns.

"Fresh out of the oven," said Chase, proudly. "My wife baked them. She's Susannah Chase."

Hovey licked his lips. The smell of cinnamon was enticing. "I know of the establishment and patronize it as often as possible."

"I would assume," said Nelie, trying to draw the secretary's attention back to her, "that you orchestrated the crowd at the harbor today."

"What? Oh, yes, Miss Belle. Messages went out as soon as Captain Stuart's first ship arrived, even as far as Goose Creek."

Nelie glanced at the door leading to the adjoining room. "Then help yourself to these sticky buns, Mr. Hovey, but could you first announce us to the governor?"

The secretary looked from the sticky buns to the girl. It took a moment for him to understand. "You wish to see the governor?" Hovey glanced at his diary. "Do you have an appointment?"

Nelie picked up the basket, took his arm, and tugged the secretary over to the door. "Oh, Mr. Hovey, when does a girl need an appointment to deliver a basket of sticky buns to her hero?"

Hovey glanced behind them. "These men are not here to see the governor?"

"I'm just making a delivery," said Samuel Chase, retreating through the door he had just come though and taking the other basket with him.

"I'm their chaperone," said Denis Belle, smiling. "Wherever these lovebirds go, I shall be there."

"So, only Miss Belle wishes to see the governor?"

"True, but I never leave her side."

"Actually," said James Stuart, looking at his future brother-in-law, "I never leave her side."

Hovey waved them off. "Then I'll escort the young lady in to see the governor. You are very fortunate, Miss Belle. His calendar is not filled for the remainder of the day. Everything was canceled when Captain's Stuart's first ship arrived."

Hovey went to the door and knocked.

When the governor asked his secretary to enter, Hovey opened the door and ushered the young woman into the governor's presence, then closed the door behind him.

Johnson scrambled to his feet. "Miss Belle, so nice to see you again." The basket caught his eye. "And what do you have here?"

Nelie placed the basket on the corner of the governor's desk and peeled back the cloth. "Sir, this is to show my appreciation for your efforts on my behalf. Until today, I never knew how much the people of Charles Town cared about my fate."

Breathing in the smell of the cinnamon, Johnson stared at the buns. "Well, they did care. Do care." Looking past Nelie and Hovey to Denis Belle and James Stuart who had entered the room, leaving the door ajar, the governor asked, "Ah, Mr. Belle and Captain Stuart, and you are here for?"

"As an escort," said Denis, smiling. "I'm not letting these two lovebirds out of my sight."

"Ah, yes," said Johnson, nodding. "Belle women do have a reputation as gentlewomen." The governor reached for the basket, and as he did, asked Nelie, "May I have one?"

"Governor, they're all yours, except for one or two for Mr. Hovey who was unable to attend my homecoming."

The governor glanced at his secretary. "Ah, yes."

"Duty . . ." started Hovey, but the smaller man was

brushed aside by Colonel Rhett charging through the open door.

Stuart caught the smaller man so Hovey would not fall into his fiancée. He righted the secretary.

Rhett glared at them. "I knew I'd find you here."

"Ah," said the governor, returning to his chair, "did you and I have an appointment, Colonel Rhett?"

"We did not, sir, but you will want to speak to me about Captain Stuart. He refuses to accompany me to Topsail Inlet."

Johnson looked at the former privateer. "Is this so, Captain Stuart?"

"That is correct. I'm obligated to Stede Bonnet for the protection he gave my fiancée while she was with those five hundred pirates."

"Further reason why you should sail," said Rhett.

"Five hundred pirates . . ." said Johnson, more to himself than anyone. Thankfully, he'd given in to Teach's demand for a chest of medicine, though it had earned him no new friends among the merchant class.

To the governor, Stuart said, "I've already told Colonel Rhett that Blackbeard will not be at Topsail Inlet."

"And as I said earlier, you cannot know that unless you have a special relationship with him."

"I do have a special relationship with Teach, and if I have the opportunity, I will avenge the insult to my fiancée."

Johnson glanced at Nelie. "Captain Stuart, I hardly think such language is appropriate with a lady present."

"Governor, I'm the only person in this room who's sailed with Teach, and when I say Teach will not be at Topsail Inlet, he will not be there."

Rhett said: "Word along the waterfront is that both of his ships are destroyed."

Stuart shook his head. "If Teach wants, he can have the *Adventure* sailing for blue water by tomorrow morning."

"You're all pirates," groused Rhett. "Or in league with pirates."

"Governor," said Denis, "if Captain Stuart is to marry my sister-in-law, and the slurs on his character persist, such as the one just uttered by Colonel Rhett, I shall fill the graveyards with bodies and Colonel Rhett shall be my first."

The governor was well aware of Belle's abilities, and in truth, after a few men had been so dispatched, one heard little about the Belle family on the streets of Charles Town.

"Governor," said Stuart, "I join my future brother-in-law in pledging that both of us would rather deal in commerce, but if we must deal with insults first, so be it."

The governor glanced at the sticky buns. The smell of cinnamon was overwhelming and these tasty morsels were getting cold. He looked up at the Scot. "Is it so important what Stede Bonnet thinks of you, Captain Stuart?"

"No, sir. It's important what I think of myself."

"And I, sir, think you are a coward," groused Rhett.

Stuart called through the open doors, "Samuel!"

Chase entered the room with his other basket.

"What's this?" asked Johnson, standing again.

"Governor, I am Samuel Chase, quartermaster of the

Mary Stewart, and I have a delivery for Colonel Rhett." Chase handed the basket to Rhett.

Rhett waved it away. "I have no time for sticky buns."

"Oh, I can assure you," said Chase, smiling, "this is definitely not sticky buns but my captain's gauntlet."

While Chase held the basket, Rhett peeled back the red flag. Under the cloth were two pistols.

He looked at Stuart. "What's this?"

"Satisfaction. Here. Now!"

In the American colonies, a portion of the merchant adventurers' booty went to the governor and certain members of the Assembly, so there was no way Robert Johnson would allow two of the most productive men in South Carolina to fight a duel. And Stuart challenging Rhett with his fiancée present . . . well, it was rather off-putting, but Johnson had to admit he'd never met a Scot who wasn't a bit mad.

Robert Johnson was the son of a former governor and considered an able and popular leader, though a bit haughty. He had arrived in Charles Town during an epidemic of smallpox and yellow fever and in the middle of the Yamassee War. Still, with Blackbeard's blockade, Johnson came to believe that here was a task he could handle: ridding the coast of pirates, but, so far, the pirates had remained stubbornly resistant in the barrier islands of the Outer Banks.

In Virginia, Governor Spotswood was negotiating with the Royal Navy to sail against "that nest of vipers," and as if to intentionally rile both governors, word had arrived that Charles Vane had joined Blackbeard for a week-long session of drinking and debauchery in Bath Town. To Johnson and Spotswood, it appeared the pirates were making the Outer Banks their new home. Bath Town was close to the North Atlantic shipping lanes and the sandbar-ridden inlets of the Outer Banks allowed any pirate a means of escape, along with plenty of empty beaches to careen their crafts.

Johnson held up a sheet of paper for both Rhett and Stuart to see. "This is a letter from Governor Eden of North Carolina. He has pardoned Stede Bonnet, Edward Teach, otherwise known as Blackbeard, and the pirates sequestered around Ocracoke Island."

Rhett said South Carolina would not stand for this.

"That is correct, Colonel. You are still going pirate hunting, whether Captain Stuart accompanies you or not. But keep in mind that we are at war with Spain again, and with this pardon"—Johnson shook the document in Rhett's face—"and Bonnet's letter of marque allowing him to attack Spanish shipping, Stede Bonnet is a legal privateer once again, so we must bide our time."

"You won't have to wait long," said Stuart, gesturing at Nelie. "My fiancée says there's little confidence in Bonnet's abilities. That means Bonnet must seize the first ship he comes across, otherwise he'll lose his captaincy as he did when Blackbeard brought him aboard the *Queen Anne's Revenge*. Pardon or no pardon, Bonnet must return to piracy. It's the only way to maintain his reputation."

A few days later, Colonel Rhett hosted a party to celebrate the engagement of Nelie Belle to James Stuart, and while the men downed drinks and told war stories—at this time, men really did have war stories to tell, as did some of the women—the ladies clustered around Nelie, offering her best wishes and admiring her engagement ring. The ring had been made in a traditional pattern, with six sets of stones to celebrate the joining of two families: birthstones of the bride's parents and the bride on the left, and the birthstones of the groom's parents and the groom on the right. As for the birthstones of James Stuart's parents, well, that took a bit of guesswork.

The party was a suggestion of the governor, who was also in attendance; everyone who was anyone was there, as well as quite a few nobodies. Also on hand was Judge Nicholas Trott, chief justice of South Carolina, and the man who would be responsible for the cancellation of the wedding between Nelie Belle and James Stuart.

But tonight was a night that brought wonderment to many, especially Catherine Belle, who could only shake her head in astonishment. All the finagling she'd done to become a member of Charles Town society and all it took was the engagement of her sister to a pirate. Who would have thought?

While everyone mingled, Nehemiah Hovey was admitted to the festivities. Once Hovey spotted his superior, the secretary posted himself against a wall and waited for Johnson to take notice. Hovey turned down a glass of Madeira but did wrap a couple of sticky buns in his handkerchief for later that night.

Sticky buns were the least of what was available on

tables filling the dining room and an adjoining parlor, as the latest recipes frequently arrived on ships from the Atlantic, the Mediterranean, or the Spanish Main; all prepared with Low Country taste buds in mind. Tables were covered with ham, chicken, turkey, and turtle; one table was filled with soups of turtle, oyster, and rice; even breads made of rice; and vegetables prepared exotically, or as simply as sliced tomatoes, a fruit still considered by some to be poisonous. And there were desserts of pudding, pies, and tarts. It was only a question of where to begin.

Governor Johnson had difficulty extricating himself from a long-winded man from Goose Creek who wanted to discuss the grievances Carolina had suffered at the hands of the Lords Proprietors.

Does the fool not think I've heard all this before? wondered Johnson. Actually, Robert Johnson had heard many of these very same grievances when his father governed Carolina, the Lords Proprietors appearing to have learned little in the last twenty years.

Once the governor succeeded in freeing himself from the Goose Creek man, Hovey whispered, "Stede Bonnet is at anchorage at Cape Fear."

"Confirmed?" asked Johnson, eagerly. Both men knew Bonnet had broken his pardon by attacking ships other than those flying the colors of Spain.

"Yes, sir. Confirmed."

The governor surveyed a room filled with great gaiety, gaiety that had been generated by the safe return of Nelie Belle. "Well, let's not spoil the party, but I would like Colonel Rhett and Captain Stuart to join me in a room where there are no ears. Cut me out of the pack when Rhett and Stuart are sequestered, just the two of them."

The four men met in an upstairs bedroom where the secretary informed the other two men of Stede Bonnet's being moored off Cape Fear.

Rhett looked at Stuart. "Then I sail at dawn."

"And I shall be there to see your ship and the *Mary Stewart* off. Never question the resolve of my crew, Colonel. They are all experienced fighters and may make a difference in a protracted sea battle. They don't know when to quit."

Rhett extended his hand and the two sailors shook on it.

"I know of your reputation as a fighter, Captain Stuart, and I wish you to understand that my previous irritation came from knowing that you would not be serving at my side."

"And I know of your reputation, Colonel, and I will be proud to serve with you in your next action."

That would not happen, and it was Nelie Belle who became the most despondent over the success of William Rhett's attack on Stede Bonnet.

TWENTY-FOUR

After a fierce sea battle in which both Stede Bonnet's ships and Colonel Rhett's ships ran aground and remained stationary, guns blasting at each other until the tide rose, Rhett was finally victorious. Bonnet was taken alive and placed under house arrest with sentries guarding him, but it wasn't long before money changed hands and a boat was furnished for his escape. The gentleman pirate had a good many friends in Charles Town. Dressed as a woman, Bonnet sailed up the coast, making it only as far as Sullivan's Island when a sudden storm blew in. Because of this, Colonel Rhett had no difficulty in recapturing him.

Bonnet and his crew were tried by a jury but without counsel, as was the custom of the day. Bonnet was interrogated by Chief Justice Nicholas Trott, and his defense was that he'd never intended to be a pirate but was overpowered by his crew. Still, the jury found Bonnet guilty, and Trott sentenced him to hang; this, despite the outcry of several prominent citizens.

Accompanied by Caesar to the governor's office, Nelie was ushered into Johnson's office. There, pleasantries were exchanged, but only the bare minimum as Nelie pleaded the case for clemency.

"I ask this in the spirit of your late father, Governor Johnson, a man who sometimes found pirates useful."

Johnson glanced at Caesar. Whatever he and the Belle girl spoke of would be all over Charles Town by nightfall—and that might not be a bad thing. "Miss Belle, those were different times. South Carolina no longer needs the goods that pirates furnished when my father held this office. Our economy is growing and your family has benefited from that growth, as you well know. Pirates are more of a hindrance to progress."

"But to hang a gentleman who went out of his way to make sure our fellow Carolinians were comfortable during the blockade, not to mention counseling patience to Blackbeard when the ransom was slow to arrive . . ." Left unsaid was the special treatment Nelie had received at the hands of Stede Bonnet.

All of this mattered little to Johnson. More than one Charlestonian suffered from a lack of medicines that had been given to Blackbeard, many of them women and children. Because of this, Johnson resolved to hang all the pirates he could lay his hands on.

Still, Nelie's pleas had not fallen on deaf ears—when it came to her sister, but for a different reason. The Belles had finally been accepted into proper Charles Town society, and now this silly girl wanted to throw all that away. Nelie didn't seem to understand that if she continued to plead for Bonnet's life, the Belle family would be looked upon with suspicion, perhaps even thought of as having something to do with the pirate's escape to Sullivan's Island.

Stede Bonnet was hanged at White Point, and it is said that the man was practically deranged before reaching his place of execution. After all, Bonnet considered himself a gentleman, and gentlemen did not suffer such a fate. Captain Kidd made the same mistake and would have been surprised to learn that once he had been hanged, his body would be placed in a cage along the River Thames as a deterrent to other sailors, gentlemen or otherwise, who considered crossing the line into piracy.

As for Nelie, she spent much of her time in church, praying for Bonnet's soul, and when she learned Governor Spotswood of Virginia had requested two pilots to lead an expedition against Blackbeard holed up in the Outer Banks, she spent more time at church than at home. She and James Stuart were to be married the next month, but as things stood, her fiancé would rendezvous with the Royal Navy three days hence.

Samuel Chase accompanied James Stuart to the church, not for propriety's sake, but because the quartermaster had turned down Stuart's request to sail against Blackbeard. The two men were still arguing the issue when it came time for Stuart to head over to the Huguenot Church. Chase had shortly returned from taking the *Mary Stewart* into battle against Stede Bonnet, and for the first time, the action had turned his stomach.

"There's nothing you can say," said Chase as they walked down Church Street. "I'm not cut out to be captain."

Or perhaps it had been the sight of Alexander's right arm being severed from the African's body by one of Stede Bonnet's cannon shots. And though the African would be properly compensated for his arm (the going rate for a right arm lost in battle was six hundred pieces of eight), Chase had been the one to step over to the cannon, fire the shot, and then, with the help of two crewmen, drag Alexander back to the cannon. There they forced the African's armless shoulder against the hot metal to stop the bleeding. Alexander screamed and passed out, and Chase returned to captaining the *Mary Stewart*, but only after tossing the severed arm over the side. Chase could still smell the burning flesh.

Chase had smelled that odor on the Main, and he had come to believe that he was pressing his luck. For that reason he agreed to accompany Stuart, Alexander, and Kyrle to Charles Town and start Stuart & Company. Not that it was all that easy for the former privateers to create a shipping line with a single ship; not to mention their main competitor was probably the source of the rumor that they used false scales heavily weighted in Stuart & Company's favor.

"You don't have to captain this mission," argued Stuart as they approached the French church. "All the navy needs is someone who knows his way around Ocracoke Island, and you've been there many times before."

"Take Kyrle. The Irishman knows those waters as well as I do."

Inside the church, they found Nelie kneeling before the altar and Caesar standing near the rear of the pews.

"No change?" asked Stuart.

"No, sir," whispered the black man. "And I have to tell you, Captain, I think she's gotten worse. Begging your pardon, Captain, but there's something wrong in that sweet girl's head."

Their attention was drawn to a figure in robes making his way up one of the side aisles. The figure stopped and motioned Stuart over to where he stood. Stuart joined the pastor in the corner, where they lowered their voices to speak.

"Your fiancée wishes that I marry the two of you at six o'clock."

Stuart didn't know what to say. He had checked his pocket watch before entering the church and knew it was just past three.

"If I marry you and Nelie before the scheduled nuptials, there will be talk. There's already some of that, you know, gossip about the relationship between your fiancée and Major Bonnet."

"Pardon?"

"Captain Stuart, you can't say you haven't heard these rumors."

"I have not. But if you'll just give me a name . . ."

The pastor shook his head. "You can't stop a rumor like this even if you marry the girl, so don't say I didn't warn you. Now follow me." But instead of going to the altar, the pastor led Stuart back to where Caesar and Samuel Chase stood near the doors at the entrance to the Huguenot church.

"Caesar, it's time to bring Dr. Rose to the church as we discussed. He and his wife should be waiting for you."

"Yes, sir," said the African, nodding more than once. "Very good. Very good, sir."

"And, Caesar, once you've fetched Dr. Rose, please bring the Belles here, all three of them, including the uncle."

"Yes, sir," said the black man, nodding again and leaving the church.

Of the quartermaster, the pastor asked, "And who are you, sir, if I might ask?"

Samuel Chase identified himself.

"Well, I can tell you there's nothing wrong with Miss Belle's nerves. I only mention this if you're the sort to suffer from a loose tongue."

The quartermaster bristled at the remark.

Stuart put his hand on Chase's shoulder. "Samuel has my complete confidence."

"Then, Mr. Chase, would you make sure no one enters the church until I return to this door. Captain Stuart and I have business to attend to."

Chase glanced at Stuart.

The Scot nodded. To the pastor, he said, "No one's coming through that door if you post Samuel outside."

"Very well."

The pastor took Stuart's arm and led him down the aisle and toward the altar where Nelie knelt in a second-row pew. When she looked over her shoulder, her face lit up, and she scrambled to her feet and opened her arms to embrace him.

For the first time in his life, Stuart felt a sense of dread, and no pirate brandishing a cutlass or a ship's cannon had done the deed. It had been a mere girl, and that girl's nightgown was pure white, had a full pleated front falling from a low neckline, and sleeves ending below the elbow. Such a gown was acceptable to receive guests in the mornings at one's home, but such a garment worn on such a sacred and formal occasion symbolized Nelie leaving her family and casting her lot with Stuart, trusting him to provide for her.

Once they had embraced, Stuart cleared his throat to say, "I've—I've been concerned about you, Nelie."

"That's silly," said his fiancée, taking his arm. "I'm the one who should be concerned. In three days you sail for the Outer Banks. Has Pastor Manigault explained that I would like to hold the ceremony tonight?"

"Yes, but I'm confused as to why." Stuart glanced to his left and right. The walls were closing in on him.

"I thought you explained . . ." Nelie could not meet either man's eyes.

"Dr. Rose is on the way," said the pastor.

That didn't help Stuart. He didn't remember a doctor being present at any wedding, but these people were French and the French were always a bit odd.

Nelie held her arms out where Stuart could examine her gown. "Well, James, what do you think?"

Stuart swallowed again and inspected the gown, spying lace here and there, especially where the bodice was cut low over the girl's breasts. "It's—it's beautiful. Is that what you're planning on wearing . . . when we wed?"

"Of course. Can Samuel stand up with you? Denis said he will fill the role of my father."

"Stand up with me?"

"There should be someone with the groom," explained the pastor.

"Well, that's a problem. Governor Spotswood has requested two pilots to assist the Royal Navy in apprehending Blackbeard, and I fear Samuel's heart is not in it, not after so many of his shipmates were killed capturing Stede Bonnet. And I have a policy of never putting a man in a position where he has to turn me down twice."

The pastor nodded as if he understood. But he did not. Samuel Chase was a Catholic, and though he and his wife attended the English church, once the service concluded, they met secretly with other Catholics to celebrate mass and wash away their sins. And with twins on the way, the Chase family was about to become even more conflicted.

"Is that the suit you'll wear?" asked Nelie.

"I guess so." Stuart glanced down. "It's the best suit I own."

Nelie laughed and looked at Manigault. "Men—always putting off everything to the very last moment."

Stuart was completely baffled. If a man asked for a woman's hand in marriage, his intended usually wanted an opportunity to draw a crowd.

"Why don't you two make yourselves comfortable?" The pastor smiled. "I doubt you need a chaperone in the house of the Lord." From his pocket, the pastor took a sheet of paper. "I'll speak with your quartermaster and give him this list. Then, I'll return after contacting those needed for the service. But you still need someone to stand up with you."

"Have Samuel locate Kyrle. He's the only Irishman I know who's a Protestant."

Manigault hurried toward the front of the church, but just as quickly he returned. "Captain Stuart, you must tell me if you're serious about marrying Miss Belle. I wouldn't want to upset other people's lives if you're not prepared to take her as your bride."

Stuart looked at the girl. "I'll marry her tonight, tomorrow, or next month. It doesn't matter when, just as long as she'll have me."

Nelie gripped his arm. "I knew you'd understand, James."

But James did not.

Once the pastor left, Nelie led him into a pew where the Scot was happy to take a seat. He needed to collect his thoughts.

As they sat there, holding hands, Nelie said, "You probably have some questions."

"Well, I did wonder why you weren't waiting until Twelfth Night, but it's understandable that you wish to be wed before I sail." Stuart glanced over his shoulder at the empty pews. "I don't think there's much chance of drawing a crowd."

Nelie's face turned grim. "They weren't coming anyway. I'm being shunned, James."

Stuart straightened up. "What?"

"It's Stede Bonnet. Didn't the pastor explain?"

"He told me there was some kind of rumor going around about you and Major Bonnet."

Nelie gripped his hand tightly. "You didn't believe it, did you? You must tell me that you didn't believe such a tale."

"I think everyone in Charles Town believes you're a woman of honor with your pleas for clemency for Bonnet."

Nelie bit her tongue. "That's what started the rumor."

"I don't understand. You spoke up for your champion. It was a point of honor."

"Well, there's men's honor and women's honor, and they are two different things."

"Nelie, we don't have to live in Charles Town. It's not the whole world."

Nelie smiled. "But it shall be our children's . . ."

Her voice trailed off as Dr. Rose and his wife came through the doors at the front of the church. The middle-aged man and his wife hurried down the aisle, and upon reaching the altar, Mrs. Rose knelt and crossed herself. Nelie gave Stuart a peck on the cheek, got to her feet, and led the Roses to a room adjacent to the sanctuary.

When the door closed, the former privateer was left alone. He looked around. The French church was one of the plainest churches he'd ever been inside, and Stuart knew his churches. On the Main, he'd sacked plenty; Catholic churches, that is.

He left the pew and paced back and forth in front of the altar, but that didn't feel right, so he walked up the aisle, opened one of the doors, and stepped outside. Strolling to the corner of Church and Queen, the feeling that the walls were closing in on him somewhat abated and his breathing returned to normal. Until this point, he'd never been responsible for anyone and now Nelie expected . . . well, it was more than just children she expected, and he'd be expected to care for them, too.

Returning to the church, he met his maid and his former cannon master. With his good hand, Alexander shook his captain's hand and congratulated him.

"Well, Captain," said the African, smiling at Julia, "I may be missing an arm, but you'll soon be missing a maid."

"Pardon?"

"I asked Julia to join me in that room you gave me over the warehouse. That's all right, isn't it?"

Stuart looked at the black woman. "I don't like losing a good maid."

"As messy as you are," said Julia, "I can understand your feelings, but it's not my place to pick your next maid. That's a job for your wife."

Stuart glanced at the church behind him. "Are you two married?"

"Oh, Captain," said Alexander with a laugh, "you know white folks don't care if us Africans marry or not."

"Well, they care about what freedmen do, and I will not give my consent for you two to live together unless you marry."

The two black people looked at each other. Julia said, "I told you he'd say that. Honor's important to them Highlanders."

Stuart ignored her comment. "What church do you attend, Alexander?"

"Anglican."

"Julia?"

"The same."

"Well, tonight you're marrying in this church."

The African looked past Stuart. "You think the pastor will marry us?"

"That's what pastors are for. They want to see all men suffer."

Julia produced a wooden box from an apron pocket. "This is why we came to see you. I didn't want you forgetting the ring."

Stuart took the box and opened it. Inside was a single gold band wrapped in white silk cloth.

"Woman," asked Alexander of his bride-to-be, "this is the small errand you wanted to run, and now I end up married?"

"I want to see my mother."

Alexander shrugged. "Fine with me."

Julia looked at Stuart. "Six? That's the hour?"

"It's what they tell me, but maybe you should be here a little . . ."

A carriage pulled up, and Catherine Belle dismounted before Caesar could climb down and open the door. Though elegantly dressed, she did not look pleased.

"Well, Captain," said Julia, "looks like your suffering is beginning a good bit earlier than you thought."

Alexander doffed his hat to the Belles, and the black couple walked down Queen in the direction of Meeting Street. They would need permission for Julia's mother to attend the service. Julia's mother was not a freedwoman.

Catherine Belle hurried past him. "I'll put an end to this foolishness."

"Well, my dear," said her husband, opening one of the doors for her, "I wish you luck."

Once his wife had disappeared through the door,

THE PIRATE AND THE BELLE

Denis Belle shook the Scot's hand. "Congratulations, Captain Stuart. You are marrying a wonderful girl."

"Thank you. But why are Dr. Rose and his wife here? Are they witnesses?"

Denis clapped the Scot on the back. "It's very simple, though I can see how the point may have eluded you. Dr. Rose is here to examine Nelie and make sure her virtue is intact. Then, after the ceremony, you are to take my sister-in-law home, lock the doors, and not come out until she's pregnant. Once you've done that, you're free to chase Blackbeard wherever he may lead you."

THE OUTER BANKS

TWENTY-FIVE

"Y̲ou're James Stuart?" asked the man sitting behind the table in the cabin of the *Jane*. He was Lt. Robert Maynard of His Majesty's Royal Navy.

"I am."

Stuart was accompanied by the Irishman, Kyrle, who wore his stocking cap. The cabin was filled with members of the Royal Navy, officers and enlisted men alike and they gave Stuart and Kyrle the once-over; the sort of look one fighting man gives another before going into battle.

"The pirate James Stuart?"

"Actually, a privateer in service to Queen Anne and now King George."

Maynard leaned back in his chair. "You sailed with Blackbeard?"

"Under Benjamin Hornigold."

"So, you took the pardon."

"Actually, I had a letter of marque. Still, I found the pardon useful. Ships of my line are rarely stopped, as pirates know I was once one of them."

A sly smile crossed Maynard's face. "And if one of your vessels was seized by pirates?"

"I'd go out and find a pirate ship and destroy it."

"Any ship?" asked Maynard, sitting up. "You wouldn't track down the specific pirate who'd stopped your vessel?"

"I have a shipping line to run, Lieutenant. I don't have time to play pirate hunter. The first pirate ship I came across I would destroy, and the best hunting is the Outer Banks. That's why Governor Johnson sent Kyrle and me."

Kyrle cleared his throat. "Actually, Lieutenant, it's only happened once, and we took no prisoners and burned the pirate ship to the waterline."

Maynard reached across the table and shook hands with both men. "I think you and I can do business."

Once Maynard had dismissed all but Hyde, who would captain the *Ranger,* the lieutenant said, "With Blackbeard at Bath Town, Governor Spotswood believes the time has come to do something about the pirate threat. The straw that broke the camel's back was a week-long party thrown by Blackbeard and another pirate, Charles Vane—you've heard of Vane?"

Stuart nodded. "Vane tried to imitate Blackbeard off the Charles Town Bar, but Colonel Rhett chased him off."

"Colonel Rhett, you say?" Maynard leveled his gaze at the Scot now seated across the table from him. "Not you, Captain Stuart?"

"Well, Lieutenant," said Kyrle, speaking once again,

"it's like this: Captain Stuart was on his honeymoon when Vane appeared off the Bar."

The other men smiled, but Stuart only stared at the deck. He'd never thought marriage could be so exhausting, but even the most cursory reading of the Bible revealed the wantonness of Eve, in or out of the Garden of Eden.

Maynard continued. "Between the crews of Vane and Blackbeard, it was a solid week of wine, women, and barbecue with rum, whiskey, and cows being furnished by the inhabitants of the neighboring villages. Eventually, news reached Spotswood and he made the decision to stamp out piracy before the Outer Banks becomes the next Port Royal."

While the English were establishing their colonies in North America, they seized Jamaica and turned Port Royal into a haven for privateers attacking shipping on the Spanish Main. It wasn't long before Port Royal became the richest city in the New World, and since most of its occupants were privateers, it also had more taverns and brothels than any other city in the Americas. For that reason Port Royal was referred to as "the Sodom and Gomorrah of the New World." In 1692, when an earthquake struck and Port Royal slid into the sea, many viewed the catastrophe as the judgment of God being rendered on such a wicked place.

Now, Great Britain was determined to wipe out piracy once and for all. That is, if they could catch them. Left unsaid was the fact that the prey was far more competent than their pursuers. Pirates could seize any ship they wanted, but the Royal Navy remained stuck with much larger crafts that were poorly manned, drew too much draft, and were bogged down in paperwork.

For example, information drawn from the hostages seized by Blackbeard outside the Charles Town Bar would take two months to reach the Admiralty in London; the first leg of a round trip, if, in fact, the Admiralty wished action to be taken. For this reason, many colonial governors purchased, armed, and manned sloops of their own. Still, chasing pirates through unfamiliar waters could turn deadly. Pirates might draw a man-of-war into a shoal over which only the pirates' ship could pass, so when the larger ship ran aground, the impact could be enough to demast the man-of-war.

Stuart had used such tactics on the Main, so there was little chance he would've volunteered for this mission if he hadn't been reassured that the governor of Virginia had purchased the proper ships. Stuart wanted to duel with Blackbeard but only on a level playing field.

"Spotswood is a very clever governor," continued Maynard. "First, he sent out spies to confirm the location of Blackbeard and then he turned to the navy for assistance. His Majesty had two ships available, but they were only useful in the open sea, so Spotswood purchased and armed two sloops that could skirt the sandbars of the Outer Banks." Maynard tapped the table. "This is one of them, the *Jane.*"

Stuart asked the question on Kyrle's mind. "I notice the *Jane* isn't hobbled by too many cannon."

"It's not that the cannon wasn't available, but Spotswood vetoed their transfer from the HMR ships."

"I like the sloop," said Stuart, reassuring the Irishman sitting beside him, "especially a fast, sleek one: a single-mast boat with sails rigged fore and aft, and more importantly, relatively shallow draft. If Blackbeard makes a break for blue water, it'll be in a sloop, and the *Jane* will do quite nicely."

Stuart did not mention the obvious: the rigid drill, the iron discipline, and the routine of the HMS sailor, all in sharp contrast with the lax attitude of any pirate ship. In battle, these professional sailors would stand and fight. It would be the pirates doing the cutting and running.

Stuart added, "I see the *Jane* has been loaded with pistols, muskets, cutlasses, boarding axes, and grenades."

Maynard smiled. "Every tool in the pirate handbook."

"Then that's the plan, to search the Outer Banks?"

"Half the plan," said Maynard, glancing at the closed door behind the two men sitting at the table. "A group of sailors and Virginia militia are marching through North Carolina as we speak. They'll attack Bath Town while our sloops blockade it from the sea. But before we blockade Bath Town, we're to round up or destroy what's left of Blackbeard's crew at Ocracoke Island."

TWENTY-SIX

Turned out it was Blackbeard anchored on the sound side of the southern tip of Ocracoke Island. Maynard knew this because he stopped every ship they came across, his two ships sailing parallel to each other and finally into the waters of the Outer Banks. Maynard timed their arrival just after dusk.

Stuart pointed at the mast rising above the dunes on the other side of Ocracoke Island. "There's the *Adventure*, and not the first ship to return from the dead."

"Does anyone see the silhouette of a lookout?" asked Maynard, peering through his glass at the dune between the *Jane* and the *Adventure*.

Those with glasses had nothing to report. Maynard ordered the lookout to keep an eye out.

"The tide?" he asked.

"Rising," said Stuart, "but these are tricky waters."

The lieutenant considered this. "Then we'll wait for morning." He looked in the direction of the *Ranger*.

"Both of us will post lookouts. Not only do we not want Blackbeard slipping away, but we don't want anyone suddenly appearing aft."

In the quiet of the evening came the sounds of a party on the other side of the island.

Stuart explained. "Blackbeard is entertaining those he does business with. I imagine there's more than one captain aboard the *Adventure.*"

"Well, they'd better return to their own ships or they're going to have the surprise of their lives come morning. What do you suppose is the disposition of Blackbeard's crew?"

Stuart stared into the inky-black water. "Probably only a sailing crew. That way he doesn't have to share his food and drink."

"Which means the *Adventure* and the *Jane* are evenly matched."

"Oh, no, sir," said Stuart, glancing at the *Jane's* mainmast where no flag flew. "You'll have the element of surprise. Even if they see us coming, they won't know who we are."

Before dawn, Maynard roused his crew, fed them a cold breakfast, and told Stuart it was time to earn his pay. Before going over the side, the Scot handed his broadsword to the lieutenant for safekeeping.

He said: "I don't think you'll have a problem with draft between Beacon and Ocracoke Islands, but when we head for the *Adventure,* you can expect to find the occasional sandbar that's shifted since the last storm."

"Just give us the soundings, Stuart."

"Aye, aye, sir." And he joined members of the crew in a longboat rowing for Pamlico Sound. From the bow, Stuart took soundings and passed them back to the *Jane*, who passed them along to Kyrle, who passed them along to the helm of the *Ranger*.

It took quite a while to bring both sloops into the channel, and by that time it was light. Those onboard the *Adventure* saw the longboat approaching and the sloops behind her. They fired at the longboat, and the shot came dangerously close.

Stuart rose up from where he was taking soundings on the bow. "Back water!" When the oars came out of the water, it was easy for the helmsman to turn the boat around. After the longboat completed its turn, Stuart shouted: "Pull, you men! Pull!"

They set a course for the *Jane*, and the crew hustled aboard while Stuart tied off the longboat so it would trail the sloop into battle. Once on deck, the broadsword was returned to Stuart.

On the *Adventure*, Blackbeard gave orders to cut the anchor chain, then ordered his starboard guns to wait until the two sloops were within range.

Blackbeard's crew waited.

And waited.

Who were these people?

As the two sloops approached, Blackbeard's master gunner, Philip Morton, loaded each of his cannons with grapeshot, scrap metal, and musket balls that would plow through the bow and into the crew on the decks of the two approaching ships.

Just for that reason, Maynard ordered Stuart and half the crew below with orders to rush topside when

Blackbeard and his men boarded the *Jane*. Stuart was not happy with the order and protested as he pulled the red shirt over his usual grey.

"Below!" bellowed Maynard. "That's an order!"

Stuart turned to go.

"What's with the red shirt?" asked Maynard.

Stuart faced him again. "No quarter, sir."

Maynard nodded. "Good signal."

And Stuart disappeared below, where each man was armed with a cutlass and a pistol, the pistols half-cocked so a premature shot would not give away those hiding in the hold.

Maynard shouted across the water to the *Ranger,* "Unfurl the colors!" and the Union Jack immediately flew over both the *Jane* and the *Ranger.*

Legend has it that Blackbeard's reply to the unfurling of the English colors was to drink damnation to the cowardly pups who dared slip up on him. He ordered Philip Morton to fire a broadside into the approaching ships.

Morton fired his grapeshot, scrap metal, and musket balls, and British sailors on both sloops went down, dead or wounded. The dead included Hyde who captained the *Ranger* and the Irishman, Kyrle, who had remained at the bow to warn the *Ranger* of an approaching sandbar. The *Ranger* was left without anyone in command and began to drift across Pamlico Sound. On the *Jane*, the grapeshot took down twenty sailors, dead or wounded.

"Fire!" shouted Maynard, and the survivors returned fire with their long guns and pistols.

There weren't that many left to return fire, but it

appeared to be enough. Small arms' fire from the *Jane* cut through the *Adventure's* jib sheet, and minutes later the pirate ship ran aground.

As smoke obscured the decks of both ships, there came the thundering voice of Blackbeard: "They're all knocked on their head, except three or four. Let's board her and cut them to pieces!"

Grappling hooks were thrown, and soon the pirates had the two ships secured, the *Jane* side by side with Blackbeard's *Adventure,* the latter ship still hung up on the sandbar. Led by Blackbeard, ten pirates leaped aboard where they found bodies littering the *Jane's* deck and the surviving members of the crew cowing in the stern.

When Blackbeard and his men rushed those in the stern, Maynard shouted, "No quarter, Teach!"

The pirate laughed. "That suits me plenty!"

And with that, Stuart and the men rushed out of the hold, firing pistols and yelling like banshees. Blackbeard and his men found themselves being attacked fore and aft. Men on both sides of Teach fell to the deck.

Out came Blackbeard's pistols, and he cut down two sailors, then recognized the man wearing the red shirt. "Stuart! You devil!"

The Scot's answer was to swing his broadsword at the pirate between him and Blackbeard. The blow severed the man's arm from his shoulder, and the return trip of the heavy sword cut the arm in half before it had a chance to hit the deck. The pirate went down, screaming, spurting blood, and trying to find his missing arm.

Maynard drew Blackbeard's attention by firing at

Teach, so another pirate stepped forward and fired at Stuart. The ball went wide, and he had both legs cut out from under him when Stuart ducked but continued to swing the broadsword. The pirate's legless body thudded to a deck quickly turning red, as was Stuart's vision. His blood lust was up, and he swung the broadsword with an old confidence, the heavy weapon feeling like a rapier in his hands.

Through the mist, Stuart saw a pirate back away. Too late. This one had his stomach opened from side to side by the broadsword, spilling guts and blood across the deck. Around Stuart, pirates and sailors slipped and fell, men writhing around on the deck or grasping whatever weapon they could find, be it cutlass, knife, or bare teeth, and fought on. But the way to Blackbeard was now clear for Stuart.

While Stuart had been otherwise occupied, Maynard had drawn first blood by a shot from his flintlock that struck Blackbeard in the chest. Teach shrugged this off, fired his final flintlock, and then threw his pistol at the lieutenant. Teach drew his cutlass and began swinging the blade in a large swath, clearing an area around him. Blackbeard was known for his physical strength, so Maynard knew this would be a fight to the death.

Once Blackbeard swung again, Maynard stepped inside the cutlass's arc and thrust his sword into Teach's chest. Luckily for Blackbeard, the sword struck his cartridge box, and when Maynard pulled back for another thrust, Blackbeard brought his cutlass around, snapping off the guard on Maynard's sword and biting into the lieutenant's fingers.

THE PIRATE AND THE BELLE

Maynard dropped his sword, stepped back, and fired his remaining flintlock. This also hit Blackbeard, but again the shot appeared to have little effect. Teach closed in for the kill, and when he raised his cutlass, James Stuart swung his broadsword, slicing Blackbeard across the face and neck.

Legend has it that the pirate faced this new threat with a compliment to the Scot: "Well done, lad."

And the Scot replied: "If it not be well done, I'll do it again."

And Stuart swung the broadsword again, severing the pirate's head from his shoulders.

Blackbeard's body collapsed to the deck, and seeing this, the fight went out of the remainder of his crew and they threw down their weapons. When Maynard and Stuart turned their attention to those on the *Adventure,* they were astonished to see the *Ranger* had rejoined the fight. Though covered with blood, and his stocking cap missing, Kyrle appeared to have locked his arms through the wheel.

"Grand gesture, if I do say so myself!"

And the Irishman's hands slipped off the wheel and Kyrle collapsed to the deck as British sailors grappled the *Adventure* and climbed aboard from the *Ranger.* Soon, pirates were begging for quarter or leaping over the side and swimming for the mainland. A few well-placed shots and the pirates returned to the *Ranger.* The captains Blackbeard had entertained the previous night had hidden below and had stopped another member of Teach's crew from blowing up the *Adventure,* per Blackbeard's instructions if his ship be taken.

Now that his fighting madness had ebbed, Stuart

slid to the deck of the *Jane*, leaned into the mast, and let the broadsword fall across his lap. As he watched, Maynard grasped the hair of the dead pirate and held up Blackbeard's head for all to see. The remainder of Teach's body was thrown into Pamlico Sound where the chilly waters had begun to turn red.

As Stuart sat among the carnage and tried to catch his breath, he heard one of the British sailors exclaim: "My God, Blackbeard's body is swimming around our ship!"

EPILOGUE

A decade later, and coinciding with the last century of the Age of Sail, Charles Town became the main stop on the Atlantic Highway. Ships leaving Europe sailed southward to the Azores to catch the trade winds to the West Indies, and from there, they caught the Gulf Stream up the coast of North America to Charles Town. For almost a hundred years, rice and cotton made Charles Town the center of the British Empire, or the new United States, until South Carolina turned inward and focused on itself, contributing to the state's decline as much as any steam-powered vessel. So, one of the best natural harbors on the Eastern Seaboard was abandoned, and occasionally revived when the country went to war. Then, one of the descendents of James Stuart, who loved sailing as much as he loved to breathe, noticed some ugly metal containers being unloaded at the port of Charleston.

While his friends at the Yacht Club derided the "soulless" containers, something tickled at the back of Stuart's mind. Soon, Stuart & Company was back in business, unloading those containers and placing them on eighteen-wheelers for the journey inland. And while most of the family had turned to the practice of the law, and their sons and one daughter attended the Citadel, this modern-day Stuart became a minor cog in the creation of the largest retail operation the world has ever known: Wal-Mart.

After appearing to be barren, Catherine Belle produced, in quick succession, five children who were raised at Cooper Hill. She was often heard to joke to her most intimate friends that there was nothing like a "good sea voyage to reinvigorate a marriage," a reference to her husband Denis's rescue mission to Topsail Inlet.

When their plantation home was completed, Catherine, Denis, and Antoine moved in. Uncle Antoine had one good year at Cooper Hill before a horse threw him while he was out fox hunting. Seven years later his son fell in a duel over a point of honor, the point of which no one appears to be able to remember what the fuss was all about.

Of Catherine's five children, four reached adulthood, and she worked diligently to turn them into gentlemen and gentlewomen. With the youngest, Catherine failed miserably. John Belle fell in love with a girl far beneath his station and moved inland to grow cotton. Later, he fought in the Revolutionary War. Another brother moved to South Georgia and married into the Wheeler family, chronicled in *Black Fire*. His descendents would fight with the Georgia Volunteers during the Civil War.

THE PIRATE AND THE BELLE

In her day, Catherine became quite the horticulturalist and even had a rose named in her honor. She lived into her seventies and was found dead in her garden with her grandchildren playing around her. Five generations later, after gross mismanagement by a series of gentlemen planters, Cooper Hill was sold to Yankees from Pennsylvania, immortalized in *The Belles of Charleston*.

Sister Nelie had one less child, three reaching maturity, but she lost all interest in Stuart & Company after her husband's ship disappeared in the hurricane of 1728. After that, Nelie turned her attention to Belle Mercantile, which had been bequeathed to one of her sons upon the death of Denis Belle. Nelie showed up for work every day until a stroke left her incapacitated and all she could do was be rolled across East Bay. From her wheelchair, and with her dead husband's spyglass, she searched the ships lying at anchorage in the harbor.

Everyone figured the old woman was waiting for the return of the *Mary Stewart*, but Nelie knew better. Her James was lost forever, but there was always the chance one of her brothers might arrive on the next ship. Unbeknownst to her and the rest of the family, the baby brother left behind in France grew to manhood on the farm where he had been adopted, and when the local priest discovered the young man had a religious calling, the boy was sent to Paris. After several rigorous years of study, the former Belle child was ordained a Roman Catholic priest, rising to the position of archbishop of Paris.

Today, Belle Mercantile still stands, however, as

Charleston has extended into the harbor, the building is now several blocks from the water and houses a micro-brewery. Samuel Chase continued to run Stuart & Company, breaking in another couple of generations of seagoing Stuarts, then retired to work in his wife's bakery. Susannah's sticky buns continue to sell well in the Historical District nearly three centuries later. Distant relation François Belle helped his sons establish rice plantations in the Georgetown area, moving from one son's plantation to the other, until one night he was found drowned in the few inches of water necessary for the cultivation of rice.

One-armed Alexander and his wife, Julia, continued to work for Stuart & Company, as they had been bequeathed the room above the warehouse. Over the generations, Alexander and Julia's descendants left the Low Country for jobs in Chicago and New York where they were shut out of the unions because of the color of their skin. It would be ten generations before any of their descendents realized that life in the Low Country might be better than life in the urban centers of the North.

Thirteenth generation Virginia Belle, called Ginny, would grow up vacationing on Pawleys Island, as depicted in *Carolina Girls*, and would later cover the Civil Rights Movement and the War in Vietnam for the Associated Press. Her niece, Mary Kate Jane Belle, a reporter for *The Post & Courier*, would track a Jack the Ripper copycat who was killing tourists in the Historical District, as fictionalized in *The Charleston Ripper*.

Governor Robert Johnson, frustrated in so many maneuvers by the men from Goose Creek, slowly saw his powers erode as revolutionaries seized control of the Assembly from the Lords Proprietors. Still, Johnson, like so many others, appeared unable to get the Low Country out of his system, and he returned in 1729 as the first royal governor when the Crown finally took over South Carolina.

So, by the end of the Golden Age of Piracy, Charles Town was no longer a frontier town bursting at the seams, but a city with a population in the thousands, endless handsome buildings, and up and down the Ashley and Cooper Rivers, quite a few manor houses with a distinctive low country flavor.

ABOUT THE AUTHOR

One of South Carolina's most versatile writers, Steve Brown is the author of *The Charleston Ripper,* a novel of suspense set in modern-day Charleston; *The Belles of Charleston,* a historical novel set in 1856; and *Carolina Girls,* a portrait of what it was like to vacation on the Carolina beaches in the sixties and the seventies. You can reach Steve at www.chicksprings.com.

BIBLIOGRAPHY

These are a few of the books I found helpful in writing this story:

Blackbeard:
America's Most Notorious Pirate
Angus Konstam

Blackbeard the Pirate:
A Reappraisal of his Life and Times
Robert E. Lee

Blackbeard and Other Pirates of the Atlantic Coast
Nancy Roberts

The Buildings of Charleston:
A Guide to the City's Architecture
Jonathan H. Poston

Charleston! Charleston!
The History of a Southern City
Walter J. Fraser, Jr.

Charleston in the Age of the Pinckneys
George C. Rogers, Jr.

The Complete Guide (Idiot's) to Pirates
Gail Selinger with W. Thomas Smith, Jr.

Conceiving Carolina:
Proprietors, planters, and plots, 1662–1729
Louis H. Roper

Dress in North America, Vol. 1:
The New World 1492–1800
Holmes & Meier

Empire of Blue Water:
Morgan's Great Pirate Army and the Epic Battle for the Americas
Stephan Talty

Everyday life in Colonial America (1607–1783)
Dale Taylor

Explore within A Pirate Ship
Paul Beck

Freedom Just Around the Corner:
A New American History 1585–1828
Walter A. McDougall

From New Babylon to Eden
The Huguenots and Their Migration to Colonial South Carolina
Bertrand Van Ruymbeke

Money and Finance in Colonial America
Charlie Samuel

Paris: The Secret History
Andrew Hussey

Partisans & Redcoats
Walter Edgar

The Pirate Queen
Susan Ronald

The Pirate Wars
Peter Earle

The Pursuit of Glory: Europe 1648–1815
Tim Blanning

A Short History of Charleston
Robert Rosen

South Carolina: A History
Walter Edgar

The South Carolina Encyclopedia
Edited by Walter Edgar

20,000 Years of Fashion:
The History of Costume and Personal Adornment
Harry N. Abrams

Under the Black Flag:
The Romance and the Reality of Life among the Pirates
David Cordingly